Book One: A Story of Reighton,
Yorkshire 1703 to 1709

Witch-bottles
and
Windlestraws

Joy Stonehouse

ISBN 978-1-913036-39-3

Acorn Independent Press

Contents

Acknowledgements

I would like to thank the helpful and friendly staff at the Treasure House, Beverley, and the Hull History Centre who made this reconstruction possible.

Also especial thanks to the members of the Hornsea Writers Group for giving their unfailing support, time and advice.

And, to Pam – the most kind and patient listener and reader that anyone could wish for – no thanks would be enough.

For Pat

Author's note

Climate change is not new. Three hundred years ago in the late 1600s, our ancestors faced what historians came to call The Little Ice Age. Extreme weather conditions continued into the early 1700s, bringing The Great Storm of 1703 and The Great Frost of 1709. The villagers of Reighton, in Filey Bay, Yorkshire, had to face severe storms, long harsh winters, heavy rain and drought. This is the story of how the Jordans, aspiring yeomen landowners, survive. It is also the story of the whole village and a traditional way of life – the blacksmith, the local healer, the vicar and the farm servants all play their parts.

While the names of characters are taken from the parish records, this is a work of fiction. The main characters, and those of higher social standing, speak in Standard English. Lesser characters and the older generation speak with a slight East Yorkshire accent.

Information about The Great Storm is taken from Daniel Defoe's account, *The Storm*, published in 1704 using eyewitness accounts.

This is the first in a series of novels that takes the Jordan family from 1703 to 1735.

Part One

The Jordans of Reighton

Chapter 1

1703

William Jordan shivered as he stepped into the dim church. It was often colder inside than out, but it wasn't the November chill that unnerved him, it was the strange winds that eddied round the village, turning almost to gale-force. They gusted from all directions and made for an inauspicious start to his friend's wedding.

He walked with the rest of his family down the aisle and saw Matthew standing to attention at the altar waiting for his bride. The sight brought a smile to his face. He wondered if Matthew was fully prepared for married life. As he shuffled along the Jordans' family pew he overheard his mother grumble with her usual authority.

'I reckon stormy winds'll make a stormy marriage.'

His father nudged her and growled in her ear. 'Dorothy – don't spoil it. If tha weds i' bleak November, only joys'll come remember.'

She sniffed and turned her attention to the flowers by the altar. William followed her gaze. The few sprigs of deep yellow gorse did little to offset the general gloom. It was so dark that morning that extra candles had been lit; they had little effect as they flickered wildly in the cold draught that flew under the door. William's mother was now twisting on the pew, trying to see old Ben at the back of the church. She began muttering under her breath.

'I see e's tried to trim 'is whiskers – must 'ave used 'is old sheep clippers.' She wouldn't be quiet. 'An' it looks like e's wearin' 'is grandfather's old breeches.'

William couldn't resist turning round to look. Old Ben had done his best, but none of his clothes matched; they were old and well out of fashion and, in some attempt to look smart, he'd stuffed a home-made neckerchief roughly into the gap at the top of his coat.

Dorothy turned back, sniffed again and looked across to the bridegroom's family pew. William sighed. He didn't want his mother to be vindictive. His family and the Smiths might be rival landowners but he'd grown up with Matthew. They were the same age, had even been christened on the same day. He'd spent many happy hours at the Smiths' and had grown to look upon Matthew's sisters as his own. Neither of the sisters was married and he thought Mary, the youngest, looked particularly attractive today. Dark brown curls escaped from the sides of her blue bonnet. Somehow sensing William's gaze, she turned her head to smile. He wasn't sure but she may have blushed a little. Just then the bride swished past and William's mother hissed into his ear.

'It's never a love match – not o' Matthew's side. 'E's after Margaret's dowry an' 'er father's land.' William knew this but couldn't vouch for the bride's feelings. He leant back on the cold pew and hoped Margaret hadn't overheard.

The vicar began the service and shouted to be heard above the wind. William tried to listen but his mother's idle gossip rang in his head, and the cold air circulating round his legs didn't help. He noticed the damp patches on the walls spreading in spite of the constant draughts, and the scent of the gorse flowers could not overcome the smell of mould and decay. He became more uneasy as the lead in the north windows rattled, threatening to cave in.

Suddenly the wind whistled through the tower and even the vicar flinched. Afraid of some structural damage, he hurried through the wedding vows. Like the rest of the congregation, he was keen to leave the church and move on to the wedding feast.

The newly-wed couple did not even stop to greet well-wishers at the church gate for the wind threatened to blow the bride's petticoat over her head. Instead, Matthew rushed to lead the way to his family's barn, though it was no easy journey. The women walked bent over, holding onto their hoods and trying to keep their gowns in place. Their menfolk guided them over fallen branches and shielded them from flying twigs as the wind grew stronger by the minute.

When they reached the barn it was a welcome contrast. Once the great doors were closed there was instant peace. They could hear themselves speak again and could rearrange their clothes and admire the decorations. Coloured ribbons dangled from the rafters, and food and ale was set out aplenty on trestle tables.

William Jordan kept his eye on Matthew's youngest sister. He'd never really thought of her as anything but a childhood playmate but, today, he had to acknowledge her as a fine young woman. As if to add weight to his thoughts, George Gurwood, the vicar, stood at the end of the barn and addressed them all.

'Marriage is the natural state for men,' he said. 'Bachelorhood is not. Once married, a man can grow in the Lord and become steady.' He turned to smile at his wife. 'Only then can a man lead a wholesome moral life. So – let us all drink to this new marriage.'

As William drank the toast, he had to agree with the vicar; George Gurwood had a loyal, healthy wife who'd already borne him seven children. Their marriage was more than steady.

The vicar's words haunted William all evening though he did nothing about them. He stayed with his brothers, equally raucous in his drinking and singing, and didn't dance with any of the girls.

That evening, the vicar wrote in the Reighton Parish Register, under the heading Marriage:-

November 23rd Matthew Smith and Margaret Watson

It was only the second wedding he'd conducted all year. He prayed it would be more peaceful than the day's weather.

Three days later, an even more violent storm hit the village.

Chapter 2

The storm was slow to reach its peak. Late in the afternoon of November 26th William was helping old Ben replenish the wood pile at the back of his cottage when, without warning, a large group of squirrels skittered up the nearby tree. Looking towards the church, he noticed rooks sailing round the top of Reighton hill like torn black rags let loose. Above the cliff, gulls battled to hold their positions. Old Ben continued to saw fallen branches despite the dust flying up and getting in his eyes. The ivy, high in the trees, pulled and tugged at the bark as if to escape; it gave William the notion he was being attacked. The wind made eerie whistling noises and rattled chains and loose boards. Ben raised his head and pointed to a flock of birds flying east. He scratched his head and grumbled aloud to himself.

'That's summat I've never seen before. Birds usually fly west i' bad weather. Lord 'elp us.'

William followed the flight of the birds towards the sea where the clouds had turned a pale gold, reflecting the sunset. He shrugged and carried on piling the logs while Ben still chuntered on about the weather. He finished helping before it got dark, and then set off for home.

When he reached the top of the hill, he had to crouch almost double against the wind. As he entered the Uphall yard he heard the horses were restless and kicking about in their stalls and, when he crossed to the house, he could swear the wind altered course and followed him. Dickon, the foreman, stepped out of the stable with Tom, one of the new lads only just arrived from the hirings. They both looked worried.

'Make sure everythin's tied well down,' Dickon ordered the lad. 'It's goin' to blow 'arder, I reckon. Oxen an' cows are gettin' jittery.'

The three of them looked warily at the bending trees and the clouds scudding by. William thought most people should be safe. The village was tucked well away from easterly gales and lay in a hollow. The church, however, was near the top of the hill and always received the full brunt of the weather. Uphall stood even higher up the hill and, although over a hundred years old, he was confident the large house was in good repair and would stand firm.

That evening the Jordan family couldn't sleep because of the wind. Neither could the hired men nor the milk and kitchen maids. In the middle of the night they all gathered in the parlour and lit candles. William's father asked him to read from the Book of Job and held a candle over the great book, mindful he didn't drip wax onto the pages. William cleared his throat and began in a loud voice.

'And behold, there came a great wind from the wilderness and smote the four corners of the house.' He could only just be heard above the wind rattling the door. Raising his voice further he continued. 'Job rent his mantle, and shaved his head, and fell down upon the ground, and worshipped, and said, Naked came I out of my mother's womb, and naked shall I return thither.'

A volley of hail clattered against the walls and windows. Everyone jumped. William fought to keep his place on the page. Out of the corner of his eye he could see Hannah, the new kitchen maid, shaking her apron up and down. His young brothers cowered and whimpered in a corner. He took a deep breath and carried on reading.

'The Lord gave, and the Lord hath taken away; blessed be the name of the Lord.'

The newly hired lads had been there less than a week and were already regretting their change of employment. They looked at the floor and thought of their precarious futures should anything happen to Uphall. William attempted to lift their spirits.

'Behold,' he read out with as much confidence as he could muster, 'happy is the man whom God correcteth: therefore despise not thou the chastening of the Almighty:

For he maketh sore, and bindeth up: he woundeth, and his hands make whole.'

His mother put her hand up to stop him. 'We can't be usin' up all these candles,' she complained. 'We're not made o' money. Get rushlights out instead.'

William sighed. He had to wait while enough rushlights and holders could be set up and lit. As he'd expected, the lights were a complete failure. Almost as soon as they were lit, a draught blew them out. They went back to the candles and William resumed his reading, but the smoke whoofing out of the chimney was catching at his throat and making his eyes sore. The wind now sounded like thunder. It tore at the thatched roof, and the rafters creaked and groaned under the strain. Determined to carry on, he shouted above the noise.

'Out of the south cometh the whirlwind: and cold out of the north. By the breath of God frost is given: and the breadth of the waters is straitened.'

In a brief lull of the wind he heard his mother still muttering behind his back about the waste of candles. There was no stopping her once she started. He gave up trying to read and suggested they all kneel and say The Lord's Prayer. It was cold on the floor, but they'd have stayed there all night if only the wind would have stopped. William's young brothers were wide-eyed with terror and now hung onto their mother's legs while his eldest sister tried to hush the baby, sobbing as if he might choke. No one wanted to go back to bed. All night they stayed close together for comfort, listening to the wind howl.

In the early morning, the wind veered to the northwest. It was now high tide and, even with their hands over their ears, they could hear the waves thudding against the cliffs and feel the house tremble. The church bells clanged as they shifted in the gusts of wind and something heavy, like a bucket, slammed into the wall.

At dawn the storm reached its peak and William's mother finally stopped going on about the candles. The wind now roared round the house. There was a sudden terrible crash above their heads. The women screamed and they all ducked instinctively. The children crawled under the table with their hands over their ears. William put his arm out to stop his mother rushing upstairs.

'I'll go. You stay here where it's safe.'

She gathered her young sons closer and kept stroking their heads as she fretted over the damage to the roof.

William soon clattered back down the stairs. 'There's a piece of chimney come through," he gasped. 'It's stuck in your bed. And there's a hole in the thatch.'

His mother began to weep but was reprimanded by his father.

'We should thank the Lord we was saved,' he said. 'Stop tha cryin'. A roof can be mended.'

She wiped her nose and tried to look grateful. As her husband bade them all kneel and give thanks, she thought about the cost of repairs.

When daylight at last filtered into the Uphall parlour, the wind began to abate. Everyone moved into the kitchen and a cold breakfast was served. No one spoke. Even William's mother was subdued. When Dickon did not arrive for his morning's instructions, they all feared the worst.

As soon as he'd eaten, William was sent out to get news. Despite the blustery wind, he found Reighton full of people wandering about assessing the storm damage. He could hear the sea still roaring as he picked his way through the debris of thatch and twigs in the main street. He realised that anyone out at sea would have been in grave trouble. Relieved to see Dickon's place still in one piece, he gave a loud knock on the door.

Isabel, Dickon's plump wife, appeared. 'Oh, William, I'm that glad to see tha face. Dickon's most upset. 'E's stuck i' bed, can't move. Come on in an' see 'im.'

William ducked his head under the lintel and followed her into the chamber where Dickon lay motionless on his back. 'What happened?' he asked.

Before Dickon could reply his wife explained. ''E were a fool to go out i' middle o' night. 'E wanted to see if 'orses was all right at Up'all.'

'I didn't get far,' Dickon interrupted. 'I were just goin' past church when a great gust o' wind sent me flyin' – bang into wall I went, right off me feet.'

'It were a good job that wall were there,' his wife said. 'I reckon tha'd 'ave ended up blown all way down to bottom o' Reighton otherwise.'

'I were pinned onto wall. I couldn't get up. I lost me lantern. It were pitch black out there.' He winced in pain. 'I think I've cracked some ribs. It 'urts when I breathe.'

'God knows 'ow long 'e'd 'ave been there if it 'adn't been for vicar an' 'is son.'

'Aye,' agreed Dickon. 'They'd come out to see church tower. I saw their lantern an' shouted, but they couldn't 'ear me at first for noise o' wind.'

'They took 'im to vicarage though,' Isabel complained. 'Per'aps to be fair, it were too windy to fetch 'im back 'ere.' She wiped a tear from her cheek. 'I were that glad to see 'im brought back this mornin'. I fretted all night.' Dickon reached an arm out to comfort her but fell back in pain.

William thought it best to leave them in peace. As he closed the door he wondered if other married couples were as devoted. He'd never seen his own parents show their feelings.

At Uphall, William saw that his father was already up on the roof and covering the hole with some tarred sacking. His mother stood below, watching with arms folded.

'We'll 'ave to 'ave someone in to mend chimney,' she shouted up. 'It's bad, all this lay out o' money. Where will it end?'

Francis looked down. 'Peace, Dorothy! There's others worse off. Why, I knows Smiths 'ave lost most o' their barn roof. I'm sendin' William an' lads round to 'elp.'

But she carried on complaining. 'I don't know why thoo's 'elpin' Smiths. They wouldn't lift a finger to 'elp us.'

He banged a fist down on the sacking as he shouted back. 'Well we're goin' to 'elp whatever tha wants. If barn i'n't mended before it rains, all their sheaves'll spoil. Thoo can't thresh all that lot i' one day.'

His mother turned away tight-lipped and looked towards the church where she could see the tower had been damaged. She also noted wisps of hay dangling from the trees and reckoned they could be saved; immediately she called to her daughters to go out and collect the loose bits.

William smiled to himself. His parents never changed but, thanks to the damaged barn, he'd be seeing a lot of Mary Smith that day.

Chapter 3

As William walked with his brothers to the Smiths' place, he saw there was a queue at the forge. Men were waiting for chisels and axes to be sharpened, and other folk were busy outside their cottages sweeping up and making urgent repairs. Usually he'd just hear the odd cow or sheep, but today it was like being at Bridlington Quay with all the hammering and banging going on. He noticed folk who hadn't spoken for ages were actually helping each other. It was the same with the Jordans and Smiths. Their envy and old grudges were put aside as the men of both families worked together and replaced the missing thatch on the Smiths' barn. They used anything to hand – whins, brushwood and straw.

When they'd finished, the Jordan boys were invited in for dinner. Matthew's two sisters, Elizabeth and Mary, served the food. All the talk was of what had happened in the night. William almost choked on his ale when he heard how Robert Storey had left his old father alone in the house to venture out and see if Elizabeth was all right. He knew Robert had been courting Elizabeth, somewhat tepidly, for years. Apart from Elizabeth, Robert shunned female company. William never understood how he could be so content to live with his old father and stay indoors to read about Protestant martyrs. To hear that a man as cautious and staid as Robert would head out in a storm to see a woman was beyond belief. Yet it was true. Robert had arrived in a panic.

'He was all of a dither,' Mary told them. 'He could hardly get his words out. Father brought him in and gave him a drink to calm him down. He didn't look very comfortable – he sat on that chair as if a ram-rod was up his back.'

Apparently, they'd all sat in the parlour till dawn, huddled together by a smoky fire, drinking warm spiced ale while waiting for the storm to abate. By morning a date had been fixed for Robert and Elizabeth's wedding. Wonders will never cease, thought William.

He kept his eyes on Mary as she walked round the kitchen helping her mother and sister. She moved with such assurance between the fire and the table. Her hips swayed under her gown. William's brothers were too busy dipping dumplings in their broth to notice his distraction, but nothing escaped Mary's sister. She nudged Mary as she put more bread on the table.

'I wish Robert would look at *me* like that,' she whispered.

Mary's face reddened. Having known William all her life, she'd not thought of him as a suitor. Elizabeth must be mistaken. Perhaps William was thinking about something else entirely while he stared at her – like calculating lengths of wood and the asking price. She watched him and his brothers finish their broth. They wiped their mouths with the backs of their hands and left without saying a word.

As the Jordans strolled home in the dusk they passed the blacksmith, now stretching his legs on a stool outside, his back against the wall. He looked exhausted. All day he'd been repairing hinges and making new fittings while being constantly interrupted by people wanting tools re-sharpened. William and his brothers didn't want to stop and talk, but Phineas hailed them.

'I 'ear Robert Storey's goin' to wed at last,' he shouted. Word certainly went round fast. 'I'm surprised. I thought 'e were too stuck in 'is ways, over keen of 'is Bible.' When they ignored him and carried on walking, he called after them. 'I pity Elizabeth if they do ever wed. She's got that much life in 'er, 'e'll suck it all out, mark my words.'

The next morning Dickon wanted to return to work but couldn't raise himself out of bed. His wife was afraid he'd done permanent damage and so went straight round to Sarah Ezard. She found her busier than usual.

'I've been rushed off me feet,' Sarah explained. 'Seems everyone suddenly wants a poultice or one o' me embrocations. An' they don't stop wantin' their cough mixtures an' stuff for achin' bones. I've 'ardly stopped.'

Isabel gazed round the room while Sarah finished filtering some dark liquid into a bottle. Pans and jars and bottles and boxes were all crammed together from floor to ceiling. Bunches of herbs hung from the rafters and blocked out most of the light, and an old blackened pot hung steaming over the fire. Isabel's nose began to itch; the room smelled of liquorice, ginger and lavender, with an overriding whiff of linseed oil. She explained Dickon's injuries and was offered one of the ready-made ointments.

'Old Ben swears by this,' Sarah said, rubbing her nose with her thumb. 'Just warm it up an' rub it in mornin' an' evenin'.' It reeked of linseed oil.

'Charge it to Francis Jordan,' Isabel said. Then she asked, 'Is there summat for all 'is pain? 'E can't sleep nor move much.'

'Take a bottle o' yon Meadowsweet. 'E's to drink it 'ot whenever 'e's badly. Tha can come back if 'e's no better in a few days.'

Isabel and Dickon enjoyed the week off work together, though he never admitted it and kept asking how things were at Uphall. Isabel spent long hours by his bedside, chatting away while she knitted or sewed and often, when it got cold, climbed into bed with him. He couldn't do much since his rib was cracked. It hurt to breathe in deeply, but they managed to kiss and cuddle gently like a new courting couple. He had time to look at her face and watch the changing expressions. He noted every move and gesture. Her skin was soft and he looked forward to feeling her lips against his. It was like falling in love again.

When he was well enough to return to work, his wife missed him and was lonely. Although he was soon back in his stride at Uphall and terrorising the hired lads, he didn't forget that special week at home.

Two days after the storm there was a tidal surge and the sea was almost eight feet higher than usual. On one of the ships sheltering in Filey Bay, the cargo had shifted. The pine, in great sawn planks, was lost overboard and washed ashore at Reighton. Word soon went round and every able-bodied man, woman and child from both Reighton and Speeton arrived to cart away the wood. They crowded round the top of the cliffs with ropes, donkeys and various sledges.

'Let's get to work quickly,' William ordered his brothers. 'It would be too cruel to gather up the wood only to get it confiscated. The lord of the manor obviously hasn't got wind of it yet.'

Both the Jordan and Smith family were there in force. Matthew began to tease William over who could load the most wood.

'Since I was baptised a few minutes before you,' he said with a smile, 'I'm the strongest. I'm the chosen one.'

William just grinned. 'I haven't a wife though to weaken me now, have I?'

'You'll find someone soon. Then we'll see who's weak.'

William shrugged and strode across the sand to grab more planks. He walked past Matthew's sister, Mary, and, for the third time in only a week, found himself gazing at her. Though small, she was very capable. He watched as she held the donkey while planks were loaded onto her sledge. It was pleasing to see her deep brown eyes and the same shy smile as her brother. The three of them had got up to all kinds of pranks when they were young. Now, here she was, an attractive young woman, holding her shawl round her head with one hand while keeping a tight grip of the reins with the other.

When he looked up from loading a plank onto her sledge, a gust of wind tore the shawl from her face. Her cheeks were flushed with the cold as she looked boldly down at him. Caught by her dark eyes, he stood still for too long in the soft wet sand and found himself sinking. His boots were soon under water. She started to giggle. Her shawl covered her face again so he wasn't sure what to think. Should he laugh or be embarrassed? What did she think of him? Why did he care anyway? He pulled his feet free and carried on with the loading.

He hauled the last planks onto another sledge and roped them down, his hands now red and raw. Then he stuffed his wet hands deep into his coat pockets and looked towards the cliff top, anxious of being caught in the act; he knew, by rights, the wood didn't belong to them.

Villagers were swarming over the cliffs and sands. From where he stood he could see all his family and more folk related by marriage or distant blood ties. Jordans were everywhere. He looked round and saw that many of the girls were now flirting. Mary's sister, Elizabeth, only had eyes for Robert Storey – their wedding would be early next year. He thought of his own future. Now twenty-three years old, he couldn't live at Uphall forever, not with five younger brothers and three young sisters. Perhaps it was time for him to move out and find a wife.

Matthew shouted at him. 'Wake up, William! Don't just stand there like a pudding- head. We've to get this timber out of the way quick.'

William saw that Mary and the others had slapped their donkeys and were making their way back along the beach to the ravine. He took a last look at the choppy sea, the grey waves flecked with white. There was more wood to be had but it was too far out. They'd have to leave it for others further down the coast. As he followed everyone up the cliff, he was glad he worked on the land; he might never make a fortune but it was surely safer than being out at sea.

Behind him he heard his name mentioned. He turned to see one of the Smiths' hired lads joking with Mary. He didn't catch all that was said but it was something to do with him being a typical Jordan, above himself and too fussy to choose a wife. They looked at him so he turned away. As the blood rushed to his face he blamed his father and grandfather; they'd kept buying more land to enclose and had rebuilt an already large house into what folk now referred to as 'the palace'. He didn't hear Mary's reply.

Chapter 4

1703-4

That night, just after sunset, everyone felt the ground shake under their feet. At Uphall, dishes and plates bounced off the kitchen shelves and all the windows rattled.

'Oh God!' shouted Dorothy Jordan. 'All me best stuff broken. Whatever next?' She began to cry and fell down in the corner with her hands over her ears for it sounded as if a coach and horses were about to crash through the door. The tremor was over in a moment, but it left them all fearful and insecure. Perhaps they shouldn't have taken the wood from the beach. Was God angry with them yet again?

Robert Storey also thought the worst. He wondered if the war with France and Spain was partly to blame and chose a relevant passage from the Bible to read to his old father.

'For nation shall rise against nation and kingdom against kingdom: and there shall be famines, and pestilences and earthquakes in divers places. All these are the beginning of sorrows.' He considered postponing his marriage, thinking he should spend more time in quiet reflection and repentance. He'd wait first and take advice from the vicar.

The Sunday following the storm and the tremor, the church was packed. Old Ben sat next to Sarah Ezard and they swapped stories.

'Me floor moved like a mat in a draught,' he said, waving his hands up and down to demonstrate.

'Aye, I can well believe it,' she said. 'I were sittin' by me fire an' I could 'ave sworn a dog were wrigglin' under me chair. Shush now though – vicar's about to start.'

17

They could only just hear the vicar speak above the wind whistling through the broken part of the roof. Odd gusts still shook the tower. George Gurwood looked stern as he gazed down on them and chose, for his sermon, passages from Nahum about God's destruction of Nineveh. He meant to frighten his flock into a hearty and sincere repentance. There was no need – they looked scared enough already. Many thought their last days had come, that the Day of Judgement was at hand. The vicar read from the great Bible. He enunciated each word and paused often to look over his spectacles to cast his eyes over certain individuals.

'The Lord is slow to anger, and great in power, and will not at all acquit the wicked.' He banged his fist down without warning and everyone jumped. 'Pride,' he said almost to himself, then repeated very loudly, 'Pride! What are we? Why, even the oak trees, once so mighty and tall and strong – they lie on the ground, torn up by their roots like flower stalks. What are we?' He turned to the Bible once more and read. 'The Lord hath his way in the whirlwind and in the storm, and the clouds are the dust of his feet.'

He closed the Bible with exaggerated care. As he looked down again at his humbled congregation he was overcome by a sense of oneness. He was no better or worse. There was Robert Storey, intense as always, frowning and leaning forward, hanging on every word. I may have been too harsh, the vicar thought. Good people have suffered with the sinful. He repeated the phrase softly,

'And the clouds are the dust of his feet.' He then paused for dramatic effect. 'What power we have witnessed, what almighty power in that wind. We all felt it. Yet the clouds are merely the dust of God's feet. What almighty power! Doesn't the tempest just cry out to all of us of God's strength, of his very existence! There is a God! And yes, he punishes. We have long provoked God's wrath against us and yes, a heavy judgement has been sent upon us. But the good news is – we can repent.' He heard a few sighs. 'We can turn to the path of godliness. And we can feel awe and a renewed respect for the Almighty.'

He smiled and opened his arms wide to encompass the whole congregation. 'We can show charity to our neighbours. We can forgive those that trespass against us. And we can be thankful. We, in Reighton, have been shown mercy.' They appreciated that and nodded their heads. 'Pray God give us the grace to be thankful and never forget his great mercy.' They joined in with a loud Amen.

George Gurwood knew very well that, by the time they reached home, they'd be thinking only of themselves again, about how much wood they could scavenge from the wrecked trees up the lane, and how they might avoid helping to repair the church tower.

Over the next few weeks, William Jordan and his brothers often gathered at the blacksmith's as news of the storm filtered through from London and the south. Phineas Wrench was the centre of attention as he passed on what he'd heard from the pedlars, fantastic tales of what was now called The Great Storm.

'Windmills,' he said, ''ad caught fire when sails blew round too fast. An' tiles from roofs 'ad been stuck deep into folk's gardens. Lead's been rolled clean off roofs an' it's not just an odd tree that's been blown down – whole orchards 'ave been wrecked.'

They shook their heads at the idea that it had rained saltwater and could not begin to imagine how hundreds of ships in London had been piled up one on top of the other in a jumbled heap.

Old Ben scoffed at the news, didn't believe half of it, but when he heard of the bodies of mariners being washed ashore below Bridlington, he thought differently. He reckoned those out at sea had fared worst; if they'd lost their rudders and anchors they'd have been helpless.

George Gurwood had a broadsheet sent to the vicarage. Among the amazing details of the storm was the sad news about the Bishop of Bath and Wells.

'He's been killed,' he related to his family, 'killed with his wife in bed when a chimney stack fell through the roof.'

It made him wonder about divine retribution and, when Robert Storey came for advice on postponing his marriage, George couldn't give any clear answers. He was less sure now about the meaning of the storm and God's purpose.

He sat in the parlour and listened with patience to Robert's excuses – his worry that he wouldn't be able to devote himself to God with a woman in the house. All the domestic chatter would distract his soul and he'd lose his way. Robert even used the excuse that Elizabeth might not want to look after his aging father. The vicar sighed. Robert was such an extreme man, so unlike himself.

'Listen, Robert,' he said gently, and quoted from the Bible, 'Whoso findeth a wife findeth a good thing, and obtaineth favour of the Lord.' The corners of Robert's lips lifted in an attempt to smile. At the vicar's suggestion they knelt and prayed for guidance, but Robert left the vicarage still undecided.

As it happened, when he spoke to Elizabeth, she ignored all his excuses and refused to wait any longer. For her, January could not come soon enough.

Robert Storey married Elizabeth Smith on one of the coldest days of the year. The church was icy. Elizabeth's sister, Mary, sat with the rest of the Smith family and looked at Elizabeth with a mixture of pride and concern. Standing by Robert at the altar, her sister looked lovely in the blue gown she'd spent ages embroidering, and her new blue cloak and hood matched the gown perfectly. She couldn't see Elizabeth's face as it was hidden by the hood, but she could see Robert plainly enough. Dressed in black, as if attending a funeral, he looked as cold and sober as the season. He didn't once look at Elizabeth but stood, immoveable as stone, his eyes fixed on the altar. She'd seen other men in his position start swaying and even faint, but not Robert – he stood firm. The church was his second home; it was where he belonged.

Despite wearing her thickest clothes, the chill of the pew bore into Mary's back and thighs. She glanced across the aisle at William. His nose was almost blue. She guessed the vicar was also feeling the cold for he kept the service as brief as possible.

After the ceremony, Mary only had time to throw her cake crumbs before Robert hustled away his new bride. He marched Elizabeth briskly down the hill to the Smiths' house, everyone else following behind. There was to be no singing and dancing in the barn because Robert didn't want it. He'd said it was enough to be feasting when they should really be fasting. Mary knew her sister would never change him. Whilst Robert was talking to the vicar, Mary approached her sister and asked if she was all right.

'Yes,' Elizabeth replied curtly. 'Why wouldn't I be?'

'Well, I know how much you enjoy a dance. This just seems a bit quiet for a celebration.'

'Look, I admire Robert for standing up for his beliefs. It's what I like about him.' Mary was not convinced. 'Don't worry about me,' Elizabeth added. 'I know him more than anyone else does. I know what I'm doing and I believe he loves me.'

As Elizabeth walked away, Mary muttered under her breath, 'And you're not getting any younger.'

Chapter 5

1704

After three days and nights of marriage, Robert Storey felt an urgent need to purify himself. As if in answer to his prayers, the vicar informed him that Queen Anne had asked for a national day of fasting for those who'd suffered in the storm. Once again everyone gathered in the church and sat on the freezing pews.

George Gurwood apologised for the cold and knew that, with the exception of Robert Storey, they'd all want a short service. From where he stood in the pulpit he noticed Elizabeth put her hand beside Robert's knee, hoping no doubt he'd take it and hold it. Robert didn't; he ignored her and kept his eyes on the altar. George Gurwood cleared his throat and read from the sheet he'd been given.

'We are to pay our respects to those who have suffered during the storm, respect the privations and losses suffered by Her Majesty's subjects. The Queen and her government ask for our deepest and most solemn humiliation.'

He put down the official paper and lowered his voice. 'You may not know it but many of our ships in the Royal Navy were blown across the sea – all the way to The Netherlands and Norway, and many sank with loss of life.' He then raised his voice. 'I've said it once and I'll say it again. We have been too proud!' He flung out one arm and pointed. 'We think the great ocean out there is our ally for trading and fishing, think it's our shield against our enemies, our protective wall.' He paused for effect. 'Well – overnight that ocean, once our defence, has become our destruction. Our great ocean is but a graveyard now. Pride!' He shouted and thumped the pulpit. 'Pride in our Navy ships, now dashed to pieces, sunk. Pride has been our ruin.'

He saw them shifting in their seats. They might have been trying to keep warm but they looked so despondent. He determined to end his message and let them go home.

'The Queen requires and God requires that we all show more humility. Please join with me today, January 19th, in a day of fasting and remembrance. Amen.'

Instead of going straight home, the men trudged across the road to the blacksmith's, keen to hear more news of the storm. They stamped their feet and rubbed their hands together while Phineas revived his fire. They watched him work the bellows until the cinders grew red.

'Come on then,' said Ben, 'fire's 'ot enough now. Tell us summat about storm.' Phineas put the bellows down at last and they gathered round to warm their hands.

'I've 'eard thousands o' trees 'ave been uprooted i' Queen's New Forest,' Phineas began. 'An' tha'll never guess – the fire at top o' Spurn lighthouse burned so fierce i' wind that the iron grate underneath it melted.' He paused, waiting for their reaction. He was not disappointed. They shuffled about and looked at each other and then back at him, eager for more. Pleased with the effect of his news, he continued. 'There's worse – 'undreds o' coal ships 'ave sunk i' River 'Umber.'

William was as shocked as the others and turned to Matthew. 'We must've missed the worst of the storm,' he said. 'We've been lucky in Reighton.'

'Aye,' agreed Ben. 'No one's been killed 'ere.'

'No,' added the blacksmith, 'an' it's odd but there's been so many tales o' folk escapin' death. Tha wouldn't believe 'ow many folk 'ave fallen through ceiling – aye, even while still i' their beds an' not a bone broken.' They shook their heads in disbelief.

'Miracles do 'appen then,' Ben mumbled.

'Do you have any funny stories?' asked Matthew. 'I mean about the storm.'

Phineas was about to relate the story of a ship floundering at sea when he realised it did have an amusing side. 'There is one tale,' he said. 'There were a ship out there an' it looked like it were sinkin' an', rather than die by drownin', captain an' ship's surgeon decided to shoot themselves. Now, funny thing was – the ship didn't sink after all. Surgeon died straight away but captain lived long enough to see 'is mistake.'

Matthew laughed. 'I must tell that to Margaret.' He looked forward to repeating the blacksmith's stories. As soon as they'd warmed up and smoked a pipe, they all went home, eager to pass on the news.

When Matthew told his wife about the sinking ship, she was not amused.

'It's not at all funny,' she chastised him. 'It's very sad.'

Until then they'd both enjoyed their conversations over dinner. Duly chastened, he tried to lighten the mood by telling her of the miraculous escapes. He also apologised for being so heartless. Though he knew full well he'd married her for the ample dowry, he was now genuinely fond of her and hated to see her upset, especially if it was his own fault. He recalled only too well the long dark winter nights before his marriage. Once tedious and, in some ways lonely, his evenings were now warm and welcoming. He looked forward each day to coming back home to his new wife. She always had hot stews or pies ready. She never complained. The house was spotless, the kitchen maid was well-organised and even the yard was clean and tidy. She was perfect and it was time that William understood the benefits of married life. With this in mind, he decided to have words with him.

The next afternoon, Matthew was working in the same field as William. He waited until sunset before shouting across the field. 'Hey, William! Come over here. See if you can untaffle this lot.'

As William wandered over, Matthew pointed to a jumble of ropes and leather straps at his feet, messed up deliberately as an excuse to talk. William raised an eyebrow. His fingers were almost numb with the cold, but he began to sort them out. Matthew helped him for a while and then elbowed him.

'If you have any feelings for my sister, I suggest you get on with it. Don't waste any more time. I can tell you, the winters are a good deal cosier with a wife to snuggle up to.' William smiled. 'Yes,' Matthew added, grinning, 'I've seen you looking at Mary – I'm not daft. And I know she's fond of you.'

William said he'd think about it.

The very next day, William put on a clean white shirt and went to the Smiths'. He found Mary in the yard throwing scraps out for the chickens. She hadn't seen him approach so he stood by the wall of the barn and watched her. He couldn't believe she was actually calling the chickens by name. Not wanting to embarrass her, he waited until she turned to go back into the kitchen before calling out.

'Mary – wait!'

She spun round to face him. 'What brings you here? Matthew won't be back till later.'

'It's you I want to see.' He walked towards her and took off his hat. 'You know Matthew's been telling me how happy he is being married.' He twisted the hat in his hands and took a deep breath. 'And I was wondering … maybe I could court you?'

She blushed and tried not to grin too broadly. 'Well, William, you'd better come inside and ask father's permission.' She led the way across the yard and into the house. Her father and mother were both in the kitchen and looked up in surprise to see William and Mary standing awkwardly in front of them. Mary nudged him.

'William has something he wants to ask you, father. Don't you, William?'

Suddenly feeling the heat of the kitchen, he loosened his neckerchief and swallowed hard. 'Yes,' he said, trying to sound confident. 'I wish to begin courting your daughter.'

'About time,' Mary's mother butted in. 'I always thought thoo'd make a good match.'

When the father nodded his head in agreement, William grew bolder. 'And I know it might sound daft, but I'd like to keep to the rules of courtship and visit once a month from now on.'

'But you see Mary all the time,' the father grumbled.

'All the same, I'd like to do it.'

Mary was flattered. 'Let him, father,' she pleaded.

So, at the beginning of each month, on a Sunday, William formally visited Mary and her parents. On his second visit he gave her a knitting sheath he'd made out of the wood from the old apple tree at Uphall. He'd carved simple crosses down the front and a heart in the middle. On later visits he gave her money and a pair of fine leather gloves. They enjoyed the afternoons spent together at her house and were both excited about the future.

'There's an old cottage down St. Helen's Lane,' he told Mary one warm Sunday afternoon in late spring. 'My family owns it. It's empty and no good anymore. Father says we can pull it down and use the cobbles to build a new place. Matthew can help if he wants. And the hired lads can be used when work's slack.'

When they walked arm in arm to look it over, her one reservation was the damp she knew people suffered there. It was something to do with the hill behind the houses. She was pleased though to see there was a decent garden at the back.

'There'll be room for chickens as well,' he said. 'And don't forget we could have a cow and a pig.'

'And can I have a kitchen maid to help me?'

'Well,' he said with a smile, 'I don't see why not.'

To William's disappointment, little work could be done on the new house that summer. All hands were needed in the fields but, every night, William walked up St. Helen's Lane to do something, no matter how small. It didn't take long to dismantle the old cottage and pile the cobbles to one side. He cleared the site of weeds and overgrown briars and tore down the ivy that was choking the apple tree. His father offered to organise the purchase and carriage of chalk stones; the house would be a useful investment. William could guess what people would say – that it was typical of 'them Jordans always gettin' above themselves'. Uphall was still the largest house at the top of the village and stood out rather grandly against the smaller cottages huddled nearby. When his father explained yet more ambitious plans for the new house, William knew that Mary would be thrilled; they'd now be getting a proper storage chamber under the roof *and* a milkhouse.

Work continued to progress slowly due to the lack of free time but, by late summer, the walls were up and William could get started on the roof timbers. The wood washed up after the storm came in useful as William and Matthew exchanged their labour for lengths of pine. By harvest time both men were suffering from the strain of working a long day outdoors and then rushing a meal before working on the house. Often they'd just grab some bread and a thick slice of ham and take it up to eat on the roof.

Mary wished she could help more and worried when William grew too lean and had a hollow look around his eyes. She couldn't imagine how he had the strength to drag himself up the hill to Uphall for just a few hours' sleep before another long day in the fields. Just before harvest time she spoke to his parents about him over-working and making himself ill. Francis Jordan wasted no time and took William aside.

'Look 'ere lad, thoo's goin' to make thassen badly carryin' on like this. Thoo's goin' to be no use to anyone. I'll see yon roof gets thatched. Don't worry. Just get tha mind on 'arvest, that's all. Mary won't want a willow wand for 'usband.' He winked and gave William a great slap on the back. 'Thoo must save some strength for later.'

William smiled and was relieved to forget the house for the time being. He could concentrate instead on Mary and the harvest.

Chapter 6

1704

During the harvest Mary helped with the reaping, but one day got up at dawn instead to help her mother bake pasties. When the food was ready she carried it up to the field and tucked it under the hedge with the kegs of beer where there was a bit of shade. She then spent the morning helping to pick up loose grains of wheat.

She kept an eye out for William but lost sight of him behind the stalks. When she did catch a glimpse she noted with pleasure the way his back arched as he bound the sheaves. His shirt, wet with sweat, clung to his back and damp curls stuck to the nape of his neck. He paused, took off his hat and wiped his face. Looking round, he caught Mary watching him. He grinned and gave her a wave. Her stomach turned over. She hoped she had the same effect on him.

She bent down quickly to continue with the gleaning, conscious of having one of the happiest days of her life. The sun warmed her shoulders and the soil under her bare feet was dry and soft. She stood up and gazed into the blue, cloudless sky and then across to the cliffs. The sea in Filey Bay was dark blue and a few cobles were sailing beyond the Brigg. She breathed in deeply as if she could absorb the day and make it part of her forever. Dickon's shouts brought her down to earth. It was time to stop work and rest.

'Allowance time! Allowance!' he yelled. The men headed straight for the beer, and William and the other yeomen helped themselves before the hired hands. Then they all sank down together and leant their backs against the stooks, grateful for the small amount of shade.

Mary and a few other women strolled over to share a bucket of water while others drank beer and shouted lewd remarks at the lads. Mary watched William as he gulped down a full pot in one go. He'd taken off his hat and his wet hair was plastered over his forehead which glistened with sweat. She sighed, realising once more how much she loved him. Some of the other women noticed her distraction.

'A watched pot never boils,' one shouted and they all laughed. Mary felt the blood rise to her face but she smiled with them. She was too happy to be embarrassed for long.

At noon everyone had more opportunity to sit and chat. They were glad to take the weight off their feet and relax, though there was no more shade to be found. Mary sat with the women apart from the men, but once they'd all eaten and had a drink, they began to mix company. Mary was going to join William but, just as she stood up to walk over to him, a few hired lads from Uphall began a bawdy song. It was full of detail and crude gestures with the deliberate intention of shocking the girls and making them giggle. Mary sat down again and shuffled behind the others to avoid attention. She did not want to be the butt of any of their jokes.

They worked through the heat of the day with just one more rest and, by late afternoon, everyone was tired. There was only the middle of the field left to cut down and any rabbits were now hiding in there. Francis Jordan and Matthew Smith stood by with guns. As soon as the women started up again with their sickles, Dickon spotted the first rabbit making a run for it. He'd hardly given the shout when about a dozen ran out.

One small rabbit hurtled straight into William's legs. He reacted instinctively. In a second he'd grabbed it and twisted its neck. It was very young and had a surprised look in its eyes. He was sorry to have ended its life on such a lovely day. He didn't believe in bad omens but hoped Mary hadn't seen it. As more rabbits were shot, others were stopped by a skilfully wielded sickle. Only a few escaped.

The lads gathered them up, tied them in pairs and wiped their hands down their breeches before going back to stooking up the sheaves. Francis Jordan kept a wary eye on them as they worked.

'Make sure tha bangs all 'eads together properly, young Tom, or they'll all topple over!'

'Aye, aye,' mumbled Tom. 'I'm doin' me best!' And under his breath he added to Dickon, "E 'as eyes i' back of 'is 'ead, that un.'

Francis heard him. 'Aye, an' I've big lugs an' all so get on with it.'

They did all get on with it and managed to finish the south field before dusk. It had been perfect harvesting weather for a change with plenty of sunshine all day and just a light breeze off the sea. They gathered up their tools and walked home, the pink sky in the west promising another fine day tomorrow. William waited for Mary and held her hand as they walked back down to the village, dawdling enough to be left behind. It was enticing the way her hips leant against his thigh and the way she held onto his hand. As they ambled down the hill, he did not want to leave her and say goodnight.

'Do you want to see how the house is coming along?' he asked.

She nodded and they continued down the hill and took the shortcut across the pasture to St. Helen's Lane. The house looked smart with its new timbers, and the white chalk walls gleamed in the twilight.

'It's all for us,' he whispered. 'Come inside and see.'

She hesitated in the doorway. 'But it's too dark now to see properly.'

'The moon's coming up soon. You'll see – it'll be light enough.'

'All right, but I mustn't be long. Father'll be wondering where I've got to. He knows we're together. He saw us leave the field.'

'Don't worry. We won't be long.' Or so he thought.

Once inside the house he was aroused by the smell of her hair, like newly mown hay, and couldn't help but stroke it, then her cheek. He opened her hand and kissed her warm, damp palm and then kissed her bare arm and her neck. Mary's heart beat faster as his lips, hot and urgent, slid under her chin and towards her ear. As he pressed closer she breathed in the manly smell of his shirt – a mixture of dry sweat, tobacco and wheat.

The moon had risen above the sea and now, large and yellow, it shone through the empty window of what would be their parlour. She looked into his face and met his serious brown eyes shining in the moonlight. There was a pile of straw on the earthen floor, left there for lining the roof. William brought her slowly down to her knees onto it, kissing her all the while. Both were overcome by a sudden need. William could hardly believe what was happening. She was so soft and giving that it didn't seem wrong to go further even though they were not yet wed. The only thing that had any meaning was their two bodies becoming one.

As they lay in each other's arms afterwards, they listened to the distant sounds of waves washing up the beach and sickles being sharpened ready for another day.

'I don't ever want to leave you,' he whispered.

'I know. Me neither.'

Later, alone in her bed, Mary lay on her back with her hands under her head. She was both entranced and alarmed at what she'd done. She didn't intend to make a habit of it but, then again, she was not the first and she'd certainly not be the last.

Chapter 7

1704

A week later, when the sheaves were gathered up, William hoped for another good day in the sun. As he worked alongside the Uphall lads he was amused by the amount of teasing they gave the girls. Tom was by far the worst. He staggered under the weight of sheaves and pretended to drop the load onto them. They were never sure when he was joking which made him do it all the more. It was Dickon who finally put an end to it.

'Enough lad. Lasses'll 'ave thoo before long. Then tha'll know about it.'

Tom gave his cheekiest grin and winked at the most well-endowed girl. William guessed Tom would have given his year's wages for the girl to have him, anyway she chose.

While William helped lift the sheaves, he stole quick glances at Mary, hoping she felt no shame about last week. He wanted the same again. It was almost unbearable the way his body responded each time he thought of that night.

As he watched her, some of the lads climbed onto the cart and sat straddled on top of the sheaves. They beckoned to the girls and hauled a few up to join them. Glad to see Mary was not one of those chosen, he joined her as she gathered up loose grains dropping from the cart. He decided to follow on foot with her and the remaining women despite Tom's jeers and the faces pulled by the other lads. He planned to walk with her once more to the new house, but Mary kept stooping to pick up grains so he didn't get a chance to speak.

It was taking forever to get to the yard. The sun was going down and no one else was in a hurry. He could tell they were all drowsy, their footsteps slowing to the rhythm of the plodding oxen. The rooks were returning to the high trees behind the church and blackbirds were singing their last songs in the hedgerows. As they neared the village he saw the fading light from the setting sun glowing on the church tower. Everything around was peaceful except for him. As soon as they reached the yard, he asked Mary to stay at Uphall for supper. He could walk her home later.

After supper, William and Mary strolled down the hill and took the shortcut again across the field to the back of St. Helen's Lane. The grass was turning wet with dew and the harvest moon had already risen above the sea. Mary, suddenly nervous, couldn't think of anything to say. She had her hopes up, but worried that last week may have not been up to his expectations. Maybe he didn't want to repeat it.

As the house came into view, William gripped her hand and ventured a kiss on her cheek. She turned her head to face him and their heads banged together awkwardly. The romantic gesture of the moment lost, they stumbled on over the damp hillocks to the rear garden. He started rambling on about the lack of progress on the house and the need to be getting on before winter set in. She, in turn, twittered about mats, pots and curtains. They walked through the dark, derelict garden and William pushed open the door.

'I mustn't stay too long,' Mary said.

'No, we'll just have a look round, and then we'll leave.'

Once inside, she gazed vacantly at the passage walls while he stood by waiting. Unsure what to say, she walked into the kitchen and looked at the unfinished hearth, then went into the parlour where the straw still lay on the earthen floor.

'There's still a lot to do,' she said, 'but I suppose we've plenty of time.'

'Did you want to marry before spring?' he asked hopefully. 'Or would your parents prefer you to wait longer?'

She took hold of both his hands and pulled him towards her. 'What would *you* like?' she teased.

'You know what I'd like.'

He kissed her full on the lips. Both knew how right they were to want an early wedding. They couldn't ignore this excitement, this sudden flaring of passion. They were young and healthy, the night was warm and the harvest was in. The bed of straw received them like a blessing.

It was over too soon for Mary who thought she could have loved him all night. She wanted to stay close and feel the weight of his body, but he rolled onto his side to see her face in the moonlight.

'I love you so much, Mary.'

Her eyes glistened with tears. 'I love you too.'

He kissed her nose, her cheeks, her eyelashes and eyebrows. He kissed her hair and neck and, when he reached her breasts, became so aroused that he took her once more. Mary was beginning to feel rather pleased with herself. This happiness, she thought, was a very well-kept women's secret. No wonder they didn't want young girls to know. Feeling smug, she thought of all the years before her.

William raised himself up on one elbow. 'And what are you smiling at, my lady?'

'Nothing. Just you.' And she kissed him to save her blushes.

'We'd better not stay here any longer, or your father'll have me strung up.'

'One more kiss and then we'll go.'

After some minutes, and with great reluctance, they pulled away from each other. They stood up, aggrieved at their separation. How could they live apart now and how could they keep their passion secret? It would not be easy.

It wasn't long before William and Mary were seen entering and leaving the house on St. Helen's Lane. Neighbours gossiped about the 'goings-on' and Robert Storey informed the vicar of the wanton behaviour. One Sunday after church, George Gurwood had words with William's father.

'As churchwarden Francis, you have a duty to uphold. Your family should lead by example. It's not right that the young should be so free with each other. If you don't check their behaviour then I will.'

Mortified, Francis Jordan warned his son to leave Mary alone. He said nothing to his wife. It was bad enough to be reprimanded by the vicar.

The warning came too late. Mary missed her monthly bleeding. She did not say anything to William until she missed the next month as well. Then, before she dared tell him, she paid a visit to Sarah Ezard. There'd be some way of knowing for certain if she was with child or not. The instructions Sarah gave were simple enough. They were not so easy to carry out though, unless you could find time alone in your kitchen.

'Boil tha first water i' mornin',' Sarah told her, 'an' let it stand in a skillet till it's cold. If bottom looks all white an' cloudy, then there's a bairn on way. If it's colour o' sand, then there i'n't.'

Mary carried out Sarah Ezard's instructions. To her horror, the urine, when boiled, looked definitely cloudy. To be sure, she tried this on different days – not an easy task in a busy house. The result was always the same – cloudy. Whenever she could be alone she bent over or jumped up and down in an effort to rid herself of the baby. She even tried lifting and throwing heavy sacks. While it was a shock to be with child, she was also rather pleased and proud that her body was working properly and could provide children for William. After failing to dislodge the baby, she braced herself to tell him.

She chose her moment carefully. She waited until they'd spent a lovely afternoon in their future garden gathering apples from the old tree. It was warm and still, quite late in autumn. Nature itself was at rest. They had three baskets piled high and were just about to take them to Uphall when she found the courage to speak.

'There's something I have to tell you.' She'd already decided that, if he was angry, she did not want to marry him. She'd have nothing more to do with him. Everything depended on how he took the news, and she'd see by the look on his face what he was thinking. Taking a deep breath, she told him straight.

'I'm with child.'

He looked wide-eyed with shock but then his face softened. His eyes were wet with emotion as he wrapped his arms round her and held her close.

'It's all right, Mary,' he whispered in her ear. 'Don't worry.'

'Don't you mind?'

'Mind?' He held her at arm's length. 'I think it's wonderful. And I think you are too. I don't know what your mother will say, though. Does anyone know?'

'Of course not. Though I think the kitchen maid suspects something. It wasn't easy boiling up my water in the morning to check it. I dread telling mother.'

'We'd better get married sooner rather than later. Let's see …' He counted out the months. 'End of June or early July, I reckon, for the baby. If we get married this winter, we'll be properly settled in our house before the birth. What do you think?'

Mary nodded. She couldn't believe her luck. It all seemed too good to be true, but the next step was to tell her mother and she must wait for the right moment.

The opportunity came a week later, on a Sunday after church. Her mother was in good spirits and they found themselves alone in the parlour after dinner. They both had their sewing out. Her mother spoke first.

'It's not like thoo to be indoors, Mary, not while it's still nice out. Thoo's not sickenin'?'

'No. But there's something I need to tell you. You know me and William want to get wed? Well, it's got to be sooner rather than later.' She waited, giving her mother time to guess the implication. 'In fact, we'd better be wed as soon as possible really.'

Now her mother had no doubts at all and looked suddenly weary and defeated. Mary thought her mother was going to cry. Instead, after pulling herself together, she said her piece.

'Well, there's worse things 'appen at sea an' worse things than 'avin' bairns. Come 'ere.' She put down her sewing and sighed as Mary knelt before her. Wrapping her arms round her daughter she held her close and, with tears in her eyes, prayed that life would be kind to her. Many a husband had changed once wed.

Chapter 8

1704-5

The next two months were spent finishing the new house. William's father arranged for cartloads of straw to be sent to the site, and Mary helped to stretch it out in layers and wet it ready for the roofing. When the thatcher arrived, one of the young maids from Uphall came to help Mary make up the bundles. Kate was strong and able. She showed Mary how to pack the straw into compact wads against her legs and how to make a good twine to tie them up. The two women were soon chatting like old friends as they took turns to wet the straw, bundle it and carry it up to the thatcher. After only a couple of days together, Mary had decided she'd like Kate to become her own servant one day.

Although the roof was thatched, William knew the days were getting shorter and the weather now was often too poor to work. It was frustrating, but the early dark evenings meant he could spend more time with Mary. He'd go to her house and sit in the inglenook where they were warm and out of the draughts. He'd watch her knitting or sewing pillowcases for their future bed. One night Matthew joined them and sat opposite. He kept them amused as he chatted about folk.

'Old Ben's been at his whiskers again with the sheep clippers. And I've been thinking about Robert Storey. His nostrils are too thin – same as his bollocks. Even the hired lads are saying he couldn't find a hole in a sieve.'

William laughed. He had beside him the two people he loved best. The firelight made Mary's eyes sparkle and gave her cheeks a healthy glow. He watched her smile, put down her knitting and fetch bread cakes to toast over the fire. They took turns with the toasting fork and then Mary spread the cakes with plenty of butter. When it melted and dribbled down William's chin, she wiped it off with her finger and licked it. That night he was more reluctant than ever to leave.

As he walked home along the frosty lane, he already missed her and felt hollow inside. He just couldn't get enough of her. If only the house was finished, then they could be married. When he climbed into his cold bed, he hunched up into a tight ball and thought how different it would be if Mary was there.

One sunny afternoon in January, William took Mary round the new house, showing off the finer points of the hearth and chimney.

'The plastering and lime-washing of the walls will have to wait till spring when the weather's warmer,' he explained. As they walked back outside he pointed with a knowing smile at the thatched roof. 'Remember our bed of straw?' She returned his smile and nodded. 'I like to think it's the same straw over our heads.' They stood for a moment and gazed upwards, their arms round each other. Everything was fitting into place.

There was one thing that Mary needed to do before she could consider the house ready to live in. When the men were out ploughing, she fetched Sarah Ezard. The woman brought with her a small brown stoneware bottle full of urine.

Mary shuddered. 'William will hate us doing this.'

'What 'e won't see 'e can't grieve over,' Sarah replied. 'Come on, let's get on with it. Pass me all that I need.'

Mary handed over a few small iron nails, a handful of human hair and some small chicken bones. Sarah put them in the bottle and stopped it up with clay. Then she tied on a piece of leather to secure it. They prised up the hearth stone, dug out a small hole and wedged the bottle in upside down, packing the earth back round it and over it. Then they laid back the flag, satisfied they'd done what was necessary to ward off evil spirits.

'Not a word, Mary. There's lots o' places i' Reighton wi' witch-bottles, but we don't talk about 'em. Best not, eh? Vicar's against it, says it smacks o' papists.' They agreed to remain silent.

On January 23rd, the day of the wedding, everyone rose early at Uphall to prepare the wedding feast. William's sister, Anna, organised the decoration of the barn, and Mary's sister, Elizabeth, arrived soon after dawn to help. William's father washed in icy water before dressing with some reluctance in fine, new worsted stockings and his best woollen breeches and waistcoat.

'An' there's one more thing,' insisted his wife. 'Don't forget tha beaver 'at.'

'Isn't that goin' too far?' he pleaded.

She raised her eyebrows. 'It's a Smith that William's marryin'. We must all look our best.'

Unlike him, she'd been planning what to wear for weeks. She'd even asked Sarah Ezard to dye her hair to look younger than Mary's mother. As a result, the previous week Sarah had been busy boiling green walnut shells and straining off the liquid.

'Mind – it's a very potent dye,' Sarah had warned. 'It must not touch owt but the hair.' It left Dorothy with beautiful auburn curls piled up above her forehead and, although it didn't quite match her eyebrows, Sarah didn't dare dye them as well.

In the upstairs bedchamber Dorothy went to the window to look out. She scraped off the frost with her fingernails. The sun had just risen and the sky had a band of pale pink clouds above the sea. It was going to be bright and sunny for the wedding – surely a good omen. Full of optimism, she put on her finest silk petticoat and the quilted woollen gown made at Bridlington using material bought years ago and saved for just such an occasion. The gown was wine-red with a dark green leafy pattern which, she thought, suited her new hair colour. Finally, she attached a fancy lace cap with a standing frill. She pulled free the curls on her forehead, teasing each one out with her little finger.

'There,' she smirked at her reflection in the mirror, 'put that i' tha pipe an' smoke it, Mistress Ann-'igh-an'-mighty-Smith.'

In the kitchen at Uphall stood a pan of Spanish wine, the basis for the posset that would be drunk after the wedding. Hannah, the eldest maid, followed Dorothy Jordan's recipe and beat in eighteen eggs and eight egg whites. She sighed at seeing all the eggs lined up. It seemed such an extravagance, especially in winter. She added the sugar a bit at a time and then grated in a little nutmeg and cinnamon. At that moment, Dorothy strode in to check on the preparations and spoke sharply to the girl.

'Tha'd best start warming it up while we're in church – but do it gently.' She wagged her finger. 'Don't let it boil! Remember – only add boilin' cream at last minute. 'As tha got it ready?'

'Aye,' Hannah answered meekly. 'I skimmed it off yesterday's milk an' saved it.' She was thinking how rich and expensive this drink was, almost a meal in itself, and wished she could have some. Just then, Matthew Smith put his head round the door looking for William.

'Tha won't find 'im in 'ere,' said Dorothy. 'There's too much fuss for 'im. 'Ave a look upstairs.'

Matthew found William already dressed and looking out of the window. William turned to see who'd come in, fearing it was his mother.

'You look a bit harassed,' said Matthew.

William sighed and pushed a hand through his hair. 'My mother's everywhere this morning. We can't go anywhere or do anything without her poking her nose in and ordering us about.'

'Fancy escaping for a while then? We could go to Ben's – see if he needs some help getting ready.'

William laughed at the idea, remembering how Ben had looked at Matthew's wedding. Eager to get away, they managed to sneak out of the house unnoticed.

When they arrived at Ben's he was busy indoors by the fire, melting beeswax to make polish. The room was full of smoke and Ben reeked of it.

'Now then,' Ben said, 'what does tha want?'

'We thought,' said Matthew, waving the smoke from his eyes, 'seeing as William's getting married today, you might need a hand.'

Ben snorted and turned his back on them. 'I'm too busy. I can see to meself.'

'That's what we're afraid of,' whispered Matthew. He noticed Ben was still wearing the shin cloths he'd worn the night before to stop his legs burning by the fire; he'd probably even slept in them. He'd probably turn up to church wearing them.

'Look,' suggested William, 'let us find your best clothes. You wouldn't want Mary to see you unfit for her wedding.'

'And,' Matthew added with a wink, 'Sarah Ezard'll be there.'

'Aye, well then,' chuntered Ben, 'I suppose I could trim me bristles a bit.'

'And we could give your clothes an airing outside,' offered William.

'Aye, all right then. Get me clothes while I finish off me polish.'

It wasn't difficult to find his clothes. Ben lived in a one-roomed cottage with only a large chest, a table, a bench and a pallet. They searched among the old clothes in the chest and scratched their heads. It was hard to see in the dim room so they took the chest outside. There were three-cornered hats, not one of them in a fit condition. There were various breeches, all grey or brown and all second-hand they reckoned.

'Ben never buys any clothes,' said William. 'He just waits for people to leave things in their will, or else he wears what his father or grandfather wore.'

'Ben,' Matthew shouted, as he rummaged about and felt something sharp, 'what on earth have you got in these breeches?'

'Oh, that'll be me moles' feet,' they heard him mumble. Then he shouted, 'I keep moles' feet i' me pockets to fend off me rheumatism.'

They continued searching through the pile. Eventually they decided on some light grey breeches that wouldn't look too odd with his father's old blue coat. His boots could be cleaned up, as could the blue hat. Ben came out and went to a wooden bucket by the door to wash his face. With a wet hand he stroked down his one remaining wisp of hair. He then dragged an old comb through his tangled beard. As he undressed they looked in amazement at something strapped round one of his thighs.

'Ben … what's that?' they both asked at once.

'It's only me dock root. This cold weather it stops me gettin' a fever.'

They looked at each other in disbelief and then Matthew suddenly burst out laughing.

'I can't go on,' he struggled to say, holding his side. 'I'm afraid to see any more. William – you'll have to finish him off.' He was still laughing as he walked away.

By the time Ben was dressed and looking fairly respectable, the church bells were ringing. William only just had time to get back to Uphall before the Jordans left for church.

Chapter 9

1705

The whole village turned out for the marriage that would join the two land-owning families. Old Ben and Sarah Ezard sat at the back of the church in their usual places.

'They've all come to gawp,' Ben whispered as he looked at folk filing past. 'They won't want to miss their share o' bride ale neither.'

'Aye, tha's right,' Sarah agreed. 'They'll gawp an' grumble. They'll find fault somewhere – an' a lot of 'em know about Mary.' She pulled a face and pointed to her stomach. 'She does look lovely though,' she added as Mary walked down the aisle to join William. Her blue dress made a startling contrast to the deep yellow of the gorse flowers decorating the front of the church. The low January sun shone through the tiny lancet windows in the south wall and caught the yellow of the gorse and the green of the carpet by the altar. Sarah thought the sun was a good sign; heaven was smiling down upon the young couple. She was about to tell Ben but the vicar began the service.

He stood tall in front of the couple and smiled before saying the customary words to William.

'Wilt thou have this woman to thy wedded wife … Wilt thou love her, comfort her, honour, and keep her in sickness and in health; and, forsaking all other, keep thee only unto her, so long as ye both shall live?'

'I will.'

Mary stared wide-eyed at the vicar as he turned to her. 'Wilt thou have this man to thy wedded husband … Wilt thou obey him, and serve him, love, honour, and keep him in sickness and health …?'

'I will.'

William's hands shook as he placed the ring on her finger. He was afraid he might faint as others had been known to do. He managed to echo the vicar's words.

'With this ring I thee wed,' he said huskily, his legs beginning to tremble, 'with my body I thee worship, and with all my worldly goods I thee endow.' They both sighed with relief when at last the vicar joined their hands together.

'Those whom God hath joined together let no man put asunder.' He pronounced them man and wife and blessed them. Matthew, as churchwarden, walked towards the altar reciting Psalm 128 as he went.

'Blessed is everyone that feareth the Lord … Thy wife shall be as a fruitful vine by the side of thine house; thy children like the olive plants round about thy table.'

Mary thought her brother rushed his reading. Perhaps he was envious. After all, he'd been married for over a year now and still had no prospect of a child. As soon as he'd finished, the vicar said The Lord's Prayer and everyone joined in. Another blessing was given and, just when William and Mary hoped it was all over, the vicar began to detail the duties of a man and wife according to St. Paul.

'Husbands love your wives, even as Christ also loved the church … So ought men to love their wives as their own bodies. He that loveth his wife loveth himself. For no man ever yet hated his own flesh; but nourisheth and cherisheth it … For this cause shall a man leave his father and mother, and shall be joined unto his wife, and they two shall be one flesh.'

Mary looked at William and smiled. She squeezed his hand as the vicar read on.

'Hear also what Saint Peter, who was himself a married man, saith unto them that are married; Ye husbands dwell with your wives according to knowledge; giving honour unto the wife, as unto the weaker vessel.'

She didn't like to think of herself as the weaker vessel. William had obviously not minded what was said; he continued to look ahead as the vicar turned to Mary and began another reading.

'Wives, submit yourselves unto your own husbands, as unto the Lord. For the husband is the head of the wife, even as Christ is the head of the Church … so let the wives be to their own husbands in everything.'

Mary thought enough had been said. She'd certainly respect and obey William so long as he wasn't violent. She shivered and realised the sun had moved and was no longer lighting the altar. Suddenly William nudged her and she turned to look at him. He gave her such a warm smile. Everything will be fine, she told herself; William is not a violent man and I'll probably get my own way anyhow.

The vicar prompted them and they kissed somewhat briefly. Then they walked side by side, still holding hands, back up the aisle and out into the bright sunshine. They stood by the porch and let people throw cake crumbs and grain over them. Smiling all the while, William's Uncle David played the fiddle and danced right in front of them like a madman, much to the shame of his daughters. Then, without warning, Francis Jordan aimed his gun high over their heads and fired. Feathers flew out and blew everywhere in the light breeze. As everyone applauded and cheered, Mary noticed her mother move towards Dorothy Jordan. She had to smile when both women almost leapt apart on seeing the colours of their gowns clash. To cover the embarrassment, Dorothy shouted out.

'Married when year is new, 'e'll be lovin', kind an' true.'

''E'd better be, or else!' muttered Mary's mother.

Mary looked up at William as he wrapped an arm round her. How could she ever doubt him? Today he looked more handsome than ever, taller somehow, and so lean and strong. She was proud to be his wife.

Francis Jordan put down his gun and stepped in front of them. He rubbed his hands together and turned to face the crowd.

'Come an' share our weddin' breakfast,' he shouted. 'An' taste a barrel o' bridal ale sent by Smiths. Everyone's welcome. Come on.' He set off down the path. The sun had dipped behind the vicarage roof and it had grown chilly out there in the churchyard; they were only too glad to leave and follow him to the barn.

Chapter 10

William and Mary entered the great barn at Uphall to find it decorated with evergreen leaves. Fresh straw lay under their feet and flowering gorse branches tied with ribbons dangled from the rafters. Mary sighed.

'I wish we could have done this in *my* family's barn,' she whispered.

'I know, I'm sorry,' he said, 'but you know what my mother's like. Once she's made her mind up, that's it. And maybe your barn was not quite big enough. I mean,' he waved his arm around him. 'Look at all this.' On one side was a long trestle table full of food. 'Your mother's obviously made up for the snub about the barn – see all this she's sent.'

In pride of place were the meats; the huge joint of cold beef and the ham were so heavy the deal planks were sagging in the middle. Set out on various trenchers and pewter plates were pigeon pies, salted herrings, mashed peas and baked potatoes. A large round of cheese was at one end of the table and a basket of polished apples stood on the floor. Tubs of butter and pots of honey and conserves were placed among the loaves of bread.

As if this wasn't enough, Tom and another lad carried in an enormous pot of mutton stew. The guests licked their lips at the sight of the oatmeal dumplings half submerged in the grease. They'd all brought their own spoons and were eager to start but waited for the vicar to propose the first toast. Seeing the guests hovering round the food, Dorothy Jordan waved a frantic arm at Tom. It was the signal for him to run and fetch Hannah with the posset.

In the kitchen Hannah had already put the four blue and grey posset pots on a wooden tray. Tom watched as she poured in the heated wine and eggs and then, with a flourish, added the boiling cream from a height. It was impressive.

A foam as white as snow welled up in the pots, almost to overflowing. When it had settled, Hannah scattered a little fine sugar over the surface and then they both hurried back out to the barn to serve it. William and Mary were to share a pot as were their parents. The vicar had one to himself. As the guests helped themselves to the bridal ale, George Gurwood stepped into the middle of the barn and asked for quiet.

'Let us drink a toast,' he announced. 'First, to the Queen. Long may she reign.'

'To the Queen!' everyone echoed. While the guests took a gulp of ale, William and Mary dipped their spoons into the posset pot and let the delicious, sweet foam melt away on their tongues.

'And now,' continued the vicar, 'we must drink to the health of the bride and groom. We wish long life and happiness to both of you. To William and Mary!'

Their names rang round the barn and a great cheer went up. William and Mary delved their spoons deeper into the posset, reaching the layer beneath the foam; they couldn't help grinning at each other as they tasted the smooth, warm custard. Francis winked at his son.

'Not bad, eh? Enjoy tha married life. Like posset, it just gets better.' Their parents began to suck from the spouts, having spooned out most of the custard. At the bottom was the heavily spiced mulled wine.

William and Mary took turns with the spout and soon felt the heat spread through their stomachs. Warmed by the wine, he put an arm round her and, as she nestled closer, kissed her on the lips. He wished he could take her home right then. Suddenly she nudged him and pointed at the guests. Everyone had gone quiet. They'd all found places to sit on the benches and were now staring at the food waiting for grace to be pronounced. As soon as George Gurwood said 'Amen' they tucked in as if they'd not been fed for months. William realised how hungry he was and dug into the food like everyone else.

After a while, William began to feel hot and over-fed. He saw that men were loosening their belts and beginning to leave the table. As Mary was busy talking to her sister and Matthew's wife, he decided to join those who'd gone outside. Once clear of the barn doors, the men loosened their clothes and took deep breaths of the cold air.

'It's good to get away,' said the blacksmith as he gazed across the yard. 'Too many womenfolk i' there for me.'

'Aye,' mumbled the others. They stood in silence for a while, enjoying the peace and the fresh air. After a while they tucked their shirts back in and smartened themselves up. Just as they were about to re-enter the barn, Matthew took hold of William's arm.

'Have you heard – the husband is the head of the family, but the wife is the neck that turns the head?'

William laughed. It could well be true. When he returned to sit with Mary, he told her what Matthew had said.

'I have heard that,' she admitted. 'We'll have to see, won't we?'

By mid-afternoon the younger guests were getting fidgety, so John Gurwood, the vicar's son, picked up his fiddle and walked over to William's Uncle David. William and Mary knew what was in his mind.

'Look,' pointed William, 'there's John making sure he plays right near my cousin Susan. He'll be wanting to show off.'

'She doesn't care for him though,' Mary informed him. 'She told me she's got enough men to put up with in her own family without looking for more.'

'Well, at least she's better than her sister. John Gurwood's after the right one. Look at Isabella sitting there as if she's sucked a lemon.'

'Isabella won't dance, you'll see,' Mary added as the music began. 'She'll be happy to just sit and gossip. But look over there.' She nudged him. 'Ben's getting up to dance.'

They laughed as Ben careered round the barn. He skipped and leapt like a man half his age. As he rushed past he left a lingering aroma in his wake. Mary wrinkled her nose as the sharp scent of smoke and fresh wax polish hit her.

'I think it's the first time I've seen him so dressed up,' she said with a grin. 'And I don't know how he manages to kick his legs up so high in those boots. They must weigh a ton.'

Finally, Ben slowed down and Sarah Ezard joined him. Within minutes, they were accompanied by a crowd of youngsters, the boys dancing as hard as they could to get rid of their surplus energy. When a romantic tune followed, George Gurwood got up to dance with his wife. Isabella Jordan nudged her sister and whispered with one hand shielding her mouth.

'There'll be another Gurwood on way after this. Just look at 'im – a church man an' all.'

Susan was not going to be drawn. 'I think they look lovely together an' I 'ope I'm like that when I'm as old as them.'

Isabella killed further talk with a stony stare and grumbled when Dickon got up and persuaded his wife to dance. ''Ow could they?' she said, forgetting to whisper. 'They 'ave no sense o' what's right, kissin' an' cuddlin' like that. Just look at 'em!'

William and Mary and the Gurwood girls, all sitting within earshot, heard the remarks. Isabella was like grey clouds on a sunny day. Mary noted that there were equal numbers of single men and women but Isabella's stern looks and sharp tongue held many back. She knew Jane Gurwood loved to dance but had not been asked. The lads, she thought, were perhaps in awe of the vicar's daughters; the girls, after all, were well-dressed, had perfect manners and could read and write.

In the end, lacking a partner, Jane asked her sister Cecilia to dance. Isabella saw them and deliberately looked the other way when they danced past. She couldn't ignore William and Mary though when they walked by to join the dance. Instead, she forced a smile, congratulated them and said how beautiful Mary looked. As soon as William and Mary were dancing, she turned to Susan, a smug look on her face.

'Tha thinks she's pure? She looks it doesn't she?' She tapped her nose. 'I know better.'

Susan was unsure whether to believe her or not. Other girls near them began to snigger. They were interested but also afraid of Isabella's tongue. If they weren't careful, she'd be spreading rumours about them.

William and Mary, oblivious to the gossip, danced past the table, weaving in and out of the others, grinning all the time. Both were excited at the thought of sleeping together in their new house, in their own bed. When the dance ended, Matthew came up to them and touched William on the shoulder.

'Now then,' he said, 'my turn. I must have the next dance with my little sister.' He twirled Mary away from him.

William staggered back to the bench more than a little drunk. He was not used to such strong drink and he wasn't the only one affected. His brothers, John and Francis, were arguing together and looked ready for a fight. Others were nodding off to sleep while his father was busy comparing the last few harvests with anyone who'd listen.

He saw Matthew's sister, Elizabeth, had got the giggles. Her husband wasn't amused, but then he never did see the funny side of things. Robert Storey disapproved of strong drink and there's nothing worse, thought William, than being stone-cold sober when you're surrounded by drunks. He was surprised though to see Robert's foot tapping under the table in time to the music.

Just then a ball of bread hit William on the cheek. Looking in the direction it was fired from, he saw Tom teasing the girls. Egged on by the other lads, Tom was busy rolling bits of bread into pellets to flick at the Gurwood girls. It was William's sister, Anna, who managed to distract Tom at last and take him away to dance. I bet she's fed up, guessed William, fed up with listening to her brothers arguing. He knew he'd drunk too much already, but people kept refilling his pot.

As the afternoon wore on and the sun went down, couples began to drift off home before it got too dark.

Matthew's wife, Margaret, said she'd go home and warm the bed. Matthew could join her later – whenever William had had enough.

Some hours later, William sat leaning his whole weight against Matthew. Mary looked around. There were hardly any women left. The barn was now very gloomy, lit only near the entrance by a few horn lanterns. William's father had been watching them and walked over to his son.

'Tha mother's 'ad them lanterns put there to get folk to borrow 'em an' leave. An' I think *thoo'd* best be goin' 'ome as well,' he hinted. 'Mary's been waitin' long enough.' He nudged him with his elbow. 'Don't want to let tha new wife down, eh?'

'No,' William managed to say. He was more than a little dazed. Mary took one arm and Matthew the other and they hauled him to his feet.

'You're in a fine state,' said Matthew. 'Some fresh air'll do you good. Come on, this way.' They guided him to the open barn door where the cold night air struck them. Matthew gazed up at the clear, starry sky. 'There's going to be a hard frost tonight. I hope Kate's warmed up your bed and got the fire well-set.'

He walked back down the hill with them to make sure they arrived safely. At the door he held William by the shoulders and looked him in the eye. 'William, listen to me. You take good care of her. She's my little sister, you know.'

Mary kicked him. 'Thank you,' she said. 'Now go home!' He lingered. 'Goodnight,' she added. 'Go on. Go home to your wife! I'll be fine, you clot-head.'

Chapter 11

The wedding night was not as William had expected. Much as he wanted to do his duty, his body let him down. What, in the past, had been reliably hard, now remained stubbornly soft. He was surprised that Mary didn't mind.

'Hush, don't worry,' she whispered. 'It's nice to just lie here together. I like talking quietly in the dark. Me and Elizabeth used to talk for ages when we'd gone to bed.' She put her arms round him and hugged him like a child. For a long time they lay like that, gently wrapped around each other. She kissed his face all over in small darting movements which made him smile. Then she talked about her plans for the garden.

'I think we could fit half a dozen chickens in there, and if we clear the bottom end I can have more space for vegetables.'

He was hardly listening anymore and couldn't keep awake. Both were aware of the old belief that whoever fell asleep first on the marriage night would be sure to die first. In spite of their fears, they both fell into a deep, restful sleep and woke in the morning still in each other's arms.

Their first month passed by like a dream. They woke early each morning to the bleating of the sheep and lambs. Mary would snuggle up behind William's back and kiss him gently until he turned to face her. Then he'd feel his way with his nose around her ears and neck and try to bury his head into her chest. He nuzzled in like a calf. When she kissed the soft chestnut hair curling over his neck, he smelled of biscuit like a warm puppy. Usually, they went to bed early and often lingered in the morning. They realised how fortunate they were to have a child on the way, unlike poor Matthew and his wife.

Away from her family, and with no close friends in the village, Matthew's wife had no one to turn to for advice. When she suspected at last that she might also be with child, she went to visit Mary. She arrived at the house to find Elizabeth there. The two sisters were giggling in the yard over something and were surprised to see her.

'Oh – you gave me a fright,' said Elizabeth, holding one hand over her chest. 'I thought it was Robert come to fetch me.'

'Sorry,' Margaret replied and blushed. It would be embarrassing to speak in front of Elizabeth who was still childless. She stood still, not knowing what to say next.

'Is there something you want?' Mary prompted.

'It's awkward,' Margaret mumbled and gestured vaguely towards Elizabeth.

'Don't worry about Lizzie. She can keep a secret. You can, can't you?'

Elizabeth nodded, intrigued by the turn of the conversation.

Margaret had no option but to continue. 'I was wondering if you knew of any way to be sure if you're with child or not.'

'Oh, Margaret! Matthew will be so pleased.' Mary grinned and rushed forward to give her a sisterly kiss on the cheek. She remembered Sarah Ezard's instructions and repeated them. 'It worked perfectly for me. I do hope there is a child for you both.' As she kissed her goodbye, she prayed that Margaret would have better luck than Elizabeth and Robert.

In late February, Margaret announced to Matthew with pride that a baby would be due next harvest. He now felt truly blessed in his choice of wife, but it was soon after this exciting announcement that she got a toothache. She never grumbled about anything so Matthew knew something must be very wrong when she suddenly threw her porridge bowl down, put her hands over her face and wept. Eventually, through her tears, she explained that her tooth – one at the back at the bottom – had been bothering her all week.

'But last night, and now … I can hardly bear it. I can't even eat my porridge!' A tear slipped down her cheek.

Matthew saw how helpless she looked. It was then he realised that he loved her. He put an arm round her shoulder and said he'd see Sarah Ezard and get something for the pain.

He returned with a meadowsweet infusion but it didn't give much relief. By midday Margaret was suffering such a severe throbbing toothache that she walked round and round the room whimpering. Matthew wanted her to see the barber-surgeon at Hunmanby, but she begged to be left alone. That evening, when Margaret's face had swollen on one side and she admitted she felt unwell, he went out to fetch Sarah. The pair of them couldn't even get Margaret's mouth open wide enough to see the problem, but Sarah suspected some badness under the tooth. Matthew wanted to blame someone.

'I bet it's all those barley sugar twists your father gave you. It's spoilt your teeth. Perhaps *he* should take you to Hunmanby and get it seen to.'

But still Margaret refused. Sarah made up a poultice of hot, moist bran which Margaret laid against her face and neck. The three of them sat round the fire staring quietly into it, waiting for Margaret's pain to subside. The swelling was now progressing to her lower jaw, her neck and even her ear. It was very difficult for her to get the meadowsweet tea into her mouth and swallow it. Matthew watched her tilt her head to avoid any liquid touching the tender tooth. After an hour, when Margaret looked more peaceful, Sarah left the house and said she'd call in tomorrow to see how she was.

Matthew and Margaret spent a long, disturbed night together. She fidgeted all the time, not knowing where best to lay her head, and often in tears with the incessant throbbing of her tooth. Her mouth tasted unpleasant, but to try and drink something made the pain worse. Matthew tried all ways to soothe her but nothing helped. He blamed himself for not making her go to Hunmanby and kicked the bed so hard in his anger that it jolted her.

'I'm sorry! I'm so sorry,' he said, ashamed of himself. It didn't matter. She was past caring and was almost wishing she was dead.

By morning, after a sleepless night, they were both exhausted. Sarah arrived with some powder of tormentil. She couldn't get it into Margaret's mouth so returned later in the morning with a decoction made from its roots. Matthew persuaded Margaret to take a few sips but she cried out when some of the liquid hit the tooth. He knew the damned tooth would have to be drawn. There was no alternative. Margaret was already flushed and feverish.

'Never mind what you saw once down some alley in Bridlington,' he told her. 'Not all barber-surgeons are butchers. I've heard the one in Hunmanby is very kind and good at his job.'

She appreciated his concern and agreed at last to have the tooth out. 'Not today though,' she struggled to say. 'I'll go tomorrow.'

Sarah looked at Matthew. Neither was happy with the delay but he shrugged weakly and agreed.

'Tomorrow then,' he said. 'Promise?' Margaret gave a slight movement of her head to pass as a nod. 'But I'll get you something stronger for the pain. I'll ride to Hunmanby for some laudanum.'

Sarah stayed with Margaret while he was gone. She got the kitchen maid to build up the fire and made another poultice. Every few minutes she tried to get some medicine into Margaret's mouth. When Matthew returned he was appalled to find his wife with a high fever, shivering so violently that her whole body shook. Her hands were icy and she complained of cold feet yet her forehead was damp with sweat. Sarah suggested they make her as comfortable as possible by the fire and warned that she mustn't be left alone. Either Matthew or the kitchen girl would have to tend to her, take turns through the night.

The kitchen maid was frightened and wanted only to fetch and carry water and cloths rather than sit with Margaret. Matthew put on a brave face as he bent over his wife and stroked her forehead with a cool damp cloth. He didn't want her to see the fear in his eyes and ground his teeth in anger at the sudden turn of events. The laudanum took effect at last and allowed her some sleep.

Relaxing back into his chair, he watched her in the firelight. It hurt to see her pretty face so distorted and swollen. His throat tightened and tears filled his eyes. He was sorry he'd brought her away from her family and friends to live in Reighton. She'd never minded and had been so good to him. He didn't deserve her. Tomorrow he'd ride to see her father and mother and get them to help. He planned how he'd take her to the barber-surgeon, which horses to use and which way to go since all the tracks were deep with mud. He cursed the time of year; it was the very worst time to be travelling. In the end he dozed off while still deciding on the best route.

When he woke up he didn't know where he was for a moment. The fire was nearly out and the room was dark and chilly. He blew on the embers and piled on some gorse. As the flames flickered he looked for signs of an improvement in Margaret. She was still clammy and only half-conscious. He tried to get her to drink some water but her tongue was swollen. As he tried again, her jaw muscles suddenly went into a spasm and locked tight. He rushed over to the maid who was sleeping in a chair and grabbed her arm.

'Wake up for God's sake! I want you to run and fetch Sarah. Tell her Margaret's worse. Tell her to come straight away. Come on – don't look so terrified. Grab your cloak and run.'

The poor girl rammed her feet into her boots and pattens and hobbled out into the dark lane. It was almost dawn. A few stars were still visible as she banged on Sarah's door.

The two women returned with a marigold infusion for the fever and some rosemary to burn on the fire, but they couldn't rouse Margaret and couldn't tell if she was breathing. Matthew stood in disbelief over his wife who now looked peaceful and untroubled. He hoped it was the laudanum faking her death, but Sarah felt her pulse and then laid Margaret's white hands gently across her chest. There was no mistaking it. They were too late. Margaret was gone.

Matthew couldn't take it in. It was too much of a shock. How could he lose so soon the love he'd found? He couldn't forgive himself. He should have done more to help. As he knelt by her bedside and buried his head in the covers, he could not believe his married life was over.

Chapter 12

Matthew's wife was buried on the first day of March and, only days after the funeral, he moved back home to be with his family. He made it clear that he didn't want any pity; he just wanted to be left alone to get on with his work. His sister, Mary, had always known when to approach him and when to let him be, but it was so different now. One Sunday afternoon she went to see him with the sole intention of drawing him out of his shell. He was alone in the stable stroking the nose of his favourite horse. She leant over the half-open door.

'Now then, Matthew.' He jumped. He'd obviously been lost in thought. 'Sorry to startle you. The horse looks in fine condition. Have you been out on him much?'

'Don't be daft,' he shot back. 'It's too damn wet and muddy.' He carried on stroking the horse, ignoring her.

She watched him as she wondered what else to say. 'Would you like to have supper with us tonight? William would be pleased.'

He turned to her with a hurt look on his face as if he'd been slapped. 'What – and spoil your happy home? No. Get back to your husband. Go on. Leave me.'

'But–'

'Just go. I'm fine.' In one stride he was at the door. He opened it and pushed her out of the way and then marched with his head down to the barn.

Matthew shunned everyone for weeks. He missed church services and avoided the vicar whenever their paths crossed. One morning, as he was on his way to the top field, Robert Storey waylaid him. Matthew stopped and braced himself for a lecture.

'Now Matthew, we all know you're grieving but there comes a time when you have to accept your lot. All that happens is God's will, don't forget.' He then quoted from the Bible. 'Touching the Almighty, we cannot find him out; he is excellent in power, and in judgement, and in plenty of justice.'

Matthew sighed and wondered how on earth Elizabeth put up with him. He could not look Robert in the eye so gazed up instead at the trees by the vicarage. They were bursting into leaf and rooks were building their nests. Looking downwards he noticed bright yellow dandelions studding the hedgerows. Signs of spring were everywhere. Only he was cold and bleak as winter. Robert droned on.

'Margaret is in heaven with the angels. Don't be so downhearted. Shall we receive good at the hand of God and not also receive evil?'

'Ha – you said it!' shouted Matthew. 'Look at you – what have you got? Nothing.' He spat on the ground. 'What has God given you? You haven't even the bollocks to give my sister a child.' He shoved Robert aside and strode on cursing the fine weather.

Throughout her pregnancy, Mary remained relaxed and in good health. Her worry over Matthew was the only cloud in an otherwise sunny springtime. When William was out for the day she was content to spend her time in the new garden tending the herbs and vegetables. William's mother sent her young servant, Kate, to help most days; the idea was that, in time, Kate could become Mary's kitchen maid. Though the two women got on well, Mary preferred the quiet times she had to herself when she could reflect on her good fortune without distraction.

One morning in early summer Mary was rather tired so stayed in bed. William got his own breakfast and left the house feeling very pleased with himself. Married life agreed with him and had put a real spring in his step. As he made his way to the fields he now understood why Dickon and the other married men winked at him.

Left alone in the house, Mary stayed in bed even longer and lay stroking the large smooth mound of her belly, awed by the miracle of the new life growing there. She gazed lazily around the room watching specks of dust float up and down in the shaft of light from the open window. Looking up at the rafters, she breathed in the smell of fresh pine and smiled at the straw in the roof. She spread her hands slowly over the bedcover, tracing the different blues of the patchwork quilt. Everything was wonderful. The sun was shining in a clear blue sky and the fresh breeze off the sea was cooling. It was perfect weather for haymaking so she knew William would be out all day and late home.

Eventually she got up and dressed, and then wandered about the garden before sitting for a while on the upturned log used for chopping wood. A robin was perched high in the apple tree and, as it sang, its bright orange chest glowed like fire in the sunlight. The whole garden was so green and full of life and hope. For some time she sat with her hands over her belly, feeling for the odd quivers of movement, and then she sauntered back indoors to wait for Kate.

In the cool of the parlour she pondered over her cooking so far. She liked to try out new ideas. Once she'd thrown a few dried currants into the bread dough and had dried some herbs and added them to the pastry for a meat pie; the pie had strange green speckles in it and there was no extra flavour but this wasn't going to deter her. She knew William thought her cooking habits rather odd but he didn't seem to mind. Today she thought she'd make oat cakes with Kate and they could try adding some honey. Days like these she wished could go on forever.

As Mary's lying-in time grew closer, she began to feel less confident. She decided to consult Sarah Ezard about her worries.

'I don't want to give evil spirits any chance of getting in and harming me,' she explained.

'Aye, tha does right,' agreed Sarah. 'Best be o' safe side. Put some nosegays under tha bed an' stuff some powdered beef under tha pillow. That should do it.'

'Thank you. William will be cross if he finds out.'

'Nay lass, 'e won't be cross. Maybe embarrassed that's all. It's not settin' a good example i' village – that's all 'e'll think. Remember – it's not 'im that's givin' birth!'

William tried to prepare himself for the birth and his gander month away. This being the first time he'd be excluded from his wife, he was rather ambivalent. For one thing he'd miss her at night-time in bed … miss her badly. Also, he didn't like the idea of all those gossips being left alone with Mary. He suspected the women would make fun of him; they'd enjoy their time away from men far too much. God knows what they said or got up to once closeted away on their own. On the other hand he'd be free to spend time with Matthew. Also, there was his mother's cooking to look forward to. Although Mary cooked her meals well and they were always ready on time, he hadn't quite got used to the strange combinations. He preferred the simpler meals and greater quantities prepared by his mother.

It was one morning in early July, when he'd already left for work, when Mary began to feel the first signs of labour.

Chapter 13

Mary paced the kitchen and passageway, waiting for Kate to arrive. She began to panic when the girl was late. As soon as Kate opened the door, Mary was upon her.

'Run and fetch Sarah. I'm having pains and the baby might be coming. Go on, hurry.'

Within minutes Sarah was there to confirm that the birthing had begun. She gave orders to Kate.

'Run an' find William. Tell 'im it's started. Then on tha way back tha'd better round up all women.'

Mary's stomach dropped as she realised she wouldn't be seeing William for some time. She was now totally in the hands of Sarah who tried to reassure her.

'Tha'll be fine. Tha mother an' Elizabeth'll be 'ere soon. An' Kate'll fetch vicar's wife. Now, Susanna's already 'ad nine bairns so if that doesn't give you confidence, nothin' will.'

Sarah made sure that Mary was comfortable before hurrying home to fetch the necessaries. When she returned, she went through the ritual of marking each corner of the house with a cross and uttered the midwives' prayer.

'There are four corners to 'er bed
Four angels at 'er 'ead:
Matthew, Mark, Luke an' John
God bless bed that she lies on.
New moon, new moon, God bless me.
God bless this 'ouse an' family.'

She then walked round the chamber checking that everything was there – candles, water and clean linen.

Mary offered a silent prayer that the labour would not be too long or painful and that the baby would live. Before long she heard the familiar tapping of the women's pattens as they approached the house. Once in the parlour, they fussed round her, smothered her with hugs and kisses and asked so many questions.

'When did pains start?'

''Ow long apart are they?'

''Ave waters broken yet?' Her sister, Elizabeth, made a move to close the window and draw the curtains but Sarah stopped her.

'No need yet. Bairn won't be 'ere yet awhile. Enjoy sunshine an' fresh air while we can, eh? Ann, dost tha want to start makin' caudle?'

Mary's mother took the hint and retired to the kitchen to prepare the birthing drink. Kate followed her to show where the ale was kept. Together they warmed it up and added sugar and spices. Kate brought it back in a large jug and poured some out for Mary first, and then the others. They drank to Mary's health. The warm, sweet ale was comforting and helped Mary relax. She drowsed as she listened to their banter.

'Might be thoo next, Lizzie,' said Sarah.

'Aye,' agreed Elizabeth's mother. 'It's about time Robert gave thee a bairn. Tha's been wed over a year an' half. 'E ought to spend same time an' energy on thee as 'e does on 'is prayers.'

Sarah looked at Susanna and winked. 'Prayers 'ave never stopped George givin' *thee* children.'

Susanna smiled. 'Prayers, like other things,' she said, 'are best done daily and kept short.' They all laughed, including Mary. She took heart from them, and a quiet, expectant joy filled the room as nature took its inevitable course.

When Mary's waters broke, the women just laughed and, when Mary's pains grew more frequent, Sarah told Kate to close the window and draw the curtains.

'Light yon candles an' stop up yon gap under door. We don't want draughts nor fresh air comin' in.' The room grew stuffy almost immediately. It being a hot day, the women's clothes were sticking to them, but it was Mary who suffered the most. Sarah leant over and wiped Mary's brow with a cool, wet cloth. She was in her element.

'Tha'd best turn over now onto tha knees,' she said calmly. 'It'll be easier.' Until then, Mary had been lying on her back, but Susanna assured her that it really was better to give birth on your knees. Mary turned over with her mother's help and faced the head of the bed. Sarah took the eagle stone from her bag and held it between Mary's thighs.

'It'll draw tha bairn just as a lodestone draws iron,' she explained as she gave it a rattle. 'Won't be long now. Cry out if tha wants Mary. Don't mind us.'

It was the last thing on Mary's mind. Her focus was only on the huge contractions of her womb. They occurred every few minutes and grew stronger, giving her less time to recover. When she began to cry out and grind her teeth, her mother rolled up a piece of linen and shoved it in her mouth. Mary had never known such agony and bit down hard on the wad of cloth. No one could have prepared her for this. There was only one thing to do – push the baby out and die in the attempt if need be. She was past caring.

She gripped her mother's hand with each contraction and squeezed so tightly her nails dug in. All the while Sarah reassured her that it was going well and told her when to push. Mary felt a sudden urge to strain with every ounce of strength she had. It hurt like nothing on earth. She thought she'd never be able to do it but Sarah and the others encouraged her. Suddenly Sarah dropped her voice and spoke slowly.

'Steady now. Wait. Now, just one more little push.' A dark, wet, sticky head emerged. Then the rest of the baby slid into Sarah's waiting hands. The blood and mess was ignored.

'It's a boy!' They all shouted. There was a tense moment as they watched Sarah clean the baby's eyes and nose. She put a tiny ball of butter in its mouth to dissolve the sticky saliva clogged there. Then at last he cried. Mary's eyes filled with tears of relief. Sarah held the baby up and invited Mary's mother to cut the navel string.

'Make it long.' Elizabeth said with a dirty laugh.

'Make it longer than Robert's, eh?' suggested her mother. She sniggered as Elizabeth blushed.

Sarah had the last word. 'It's not size that matters but what tha does with it. Cut it 'ow long tha likes, Ann.'

Once the cord was clamped and cut, Sarah tied it, washed the baby and wrapped him tightly in swaddling cloths. The baby stopped crying and appeared to look round the dimly lit room. He was handed to Mary, now lying on her back again. She looked in amazement at the tiny dark-haired baby.

'Little Thomas,' she whispered to him. The others overheard and were shocked.

'Doesn't tha know?' said Kate. 'It's bad luck to say bairn's name before baptism.' Her words were like a slap of cold water.

Elizabeth tried to make amends. 'She only whispered it to the bairn. Not to us.'

'Aye. Well. Maybe that'll save it. Maybe not. It's i' Lord's 'ands. Lord giveth–'

'Aye Kate, we know,' interrupted Sarah as she finished washing her hands.

Susanna suggested they all join her in prayer so they hitched up their gowns and knelt in a semi-circle at the foot of the bed. 'Father, we thank thee for blessing us with the safe deliverance of a new child. We are, as ever, poor sinners greatly in thy debt. Help us in all our doings to honour thy name and do thy will. Amen.'

Mary was close to tears but Elizabeth winked at her and stepped closer to admire the baby in more detail. 'He's lovely, Mary. Just look at those eyebrows and all that hair. He'll break a few hearts.'

'Do you think he'll be all right?'

'Of course he will. Don't worry. You rest now. We'll do everything.' She turned to the others. 'We're Mary's servants and slaves now. Aren't we?'

'Aye Mary,' said her mother, 'we're at *thy* beck an' call now for a change. Make on – tha lyin'-in month'll be over sooner than tha thinks. Put bairn to tha breast. See if 'e'll drink.'

The baby made a vague attempt to suck at the nipple and then gave up, but it was enough to stimulate the afterbirth to come away. Sarah pressed down firmly on Mary's stomach to make sure any other remains were expelled. As Kate cleared away the linen, now sodden with water and blood, she wrinkled her nose up. It was the first birth she'd witnessed and the iron-rich smell of the blood got into her throat and made her retch. Sarah grabbed her by the arm, pulled her aside and whispered through clenched teeth.

'Thoo's got a job to do so do it. Make sure tha buries afterbirth deep i' garden – deep enough so nowt can find it.'

Mary watched Kate leave and then felt suddenly so tired and heavy, as if her body might sink right through the bed. She handed the baby to her mother and watched as she lowered him gently into the old Jordan crib. The dark, polished oak panels shone in the candlelight. It pleased Mary to think that William had slept in the same crib. She nudged it with her toe to set it rocking.

'William will be so proud to have a son,' she murmured. 'Can someone go and tell him?'

'I'll go,' offered Elizabeth. 'He'll be in the hay meadow. Do you want me to say anything special?'

'No, just that I'm well and ... no, just say I'm well.'

'Very good, if you're sure that's all. I'll see you later.'

The women sensed that Mary needed to rest so everyone except Sarah left the room and busied themselves in the kitchen preparing dinner. It was so peaceful now as Sarah began the ritual cleansing. Mary basked under the gentle pressure of the warm damp cloth as it moved slowly over every part of her body. It made her think she'd earned this loving attention, like a hero after some great battle.

Meanwhile, Elizabeth was rushing down Oxtrope Lane towards the hay field, holding her skirts up so she could run faster. She could hear everyone in the field ahead long before she saw them. The villagers were turning over the mown grass, making the best of the fine weather.

William saw her out of the corner of his eye. He dropped his rake and his heart stopped. His mouth went dry as he feared bad news.

Elizabeth saw his worried face so shouted as she ran closer. 'It's a boy! William, it's a boy! You have a son.' William ran to meet her. 'It's a boy!' she repeated out of breath. 'And Mary's doing fine.'

'It's a boy!' He shouted back to the others. They cheered and downed tools to congratulate him. The women wanted more news of the birth and wandered aside to get all the details from Elizabeth while the men patted William on the back and gave him advice.

'Don't let women make a sop of 'im. Treat 'im tough,' offered Ben.

'Make most o' tha month away,' advised his uncle, 'tha'll soon 'ave enough o' women an' bairns before long.'

Dickon was more sympathetic. 'Well done, lad. I 'ope tha'll be very 'appy.'

William's father waited until the noise and excitement had died down and everyone had gone back to work. 'It's wonderful news, William. Lord be praised.'

'Thanks. I don't know what to say. I have no words.'

'I expect tha's decided on godparents? I'll see vicar about baptism.'

Elizabeth saw that her brother Matthew was hanging back. She called him over and, with some reluctance, he approached William. He forced a smile and gave William a shove.

'You lucky devil!'

'Well, you're doing very well with your family's land,' William mumbled.

'Ay, that's true. Give me another twenty years and I'll be lord of a lot more of this.' Matthew waved his arm to encompass the whole area.

William realised that, without a child of his own, Matthew's ambitions might now be centred solely on farming. Some Jordan land had been conveyed cheaply to him in the spring on account of all his help with the new house; what with the remains of his wife's dowry still to spend, Matthew's future did look more promising in one respect at least.

As Matthew went back to raking the grass, Elizabeth thought he looked sad. She went up to him and put a hand on his shoulder but he shrugged her off.

'No doubt you'll be spending half your time with Mary and the new bairn now,' he complained. 'Won't see you at all.'

'That's not fair. You know you're more than welcome to come round any evening. I'm sure Robert will be glad to see you.'

'No,' he spat. 'I get more than enough prayers and Bible readings on Sundays.'

'Oh, Matthew. You can't go on blaming God forever.'

'That's my affair,' he replied. 'Leave me be.'

Chapter 14

Mary soon fell into a deep sleep and awoke later to find a crowd of women in the parlour. They'd made her some porridge and toast and sat around chatting while she ate. William's mother had brought some blue woollen threads plaited into a necklace.

''Ere,' she said to Mary, 'wear this round tha neck. It'll stop tha gettin' milk fever.' Mary played with it in her hands and thanked her. She hadn't even fed the baby properly, let alone thought of what could go wrong. As her mother-in-law moved away, Mary overheard her complaining to the others.

'Don't know why she 'ad to give birth in 'er bed. What's wrong wi' straw o' kitchen floor? It always suited me well enough.'

Elizabeth bit her lip. There was so much she'd like to have said to Dorothy Jordan. Instead, she sat on the bed.

'Come on, cheer up,' she said to Mary. 'You should've seen William's eyes light up when he heard he had a son! And everyone's so happy for you both.' Mary smiled, grateful for her sister's sympathy.

After a while, Sarah realised that Mary was getting tired. She reminded them that Mary must stay in bed for a few days' rest and not have too many visitors.

Mary delighted in her first day with the baby. It was peaceful in the parlour and all she need do was look at her son and feed him. The next day though, when she was passing water, she suddenly went weak and shaky. The reason for this was soon apparent as a large hot clot of blood fell into the bed pan. More blood came – like a dark red jelly. She almost fainted at the sight of it. Kate panicked and ran to get help. Sarah Ezard would say if it was normal or not and know what to do.

Sarah rushed to the house and shouted out orders. 'Kate, fetch some 'ot water an' cloths. Mary, thoo must just lie still. It'll be all right.' Once Kate had brought in the hot water and cloths and had disappeared again into the kitchen, Sarah rested her hands on Mary's womb and pressed down. Mary winced, more through fear than pain, and more hot liquid ran between her thighs. Sarah cleared away the bloodied sheet, washed Mary's legs and told her she'd be fine now.

'Last of afterbirth 'as come away,' she explained, 'an' unless there's more bleedin', tha needn't worry. Just rest. Don't strain thassen. Remember, we're 'ere to do everythin' for thee. Enjoy a bit more peace an' quiet. Just love tha baby an' do carry on tryin' to feed 'im. I know it's not easy at first.'

That was the problem. The baby was small which meant he couldn't take much milk at a time. This led to over-frequent feeds and Mary's breasts were beginning to get sore.

In a couple more days, Mary was allowed to sit up in bed. She believed she could get used to this lying-in routine. She need only think about herself and baby Thomas, spend her idle time gazing at his tiny fingernails whenever he was unwrapped, his snubbed nose and arched eyebrows, wondering what colour those dark blue eyes would become. Who was he like? Would his hair grow curly? Would he be strong? Would he take after the Smiths or the Jordans? There was always some woman visiting to break up her thoughts. As well as Sarah and Dorothy Jordan, her mother and sister came daily and they often brought others.

After a week of lying in bed in the darkened room, Mary grew restless. She could hear the summer noises outside, men shouting to their horses and oxen on their way to and from the fields, the clopping of hooves on the dry, hard road, birds singing, children running by and women chattering as they fetched water from the well. She missed being out in the sunshine, and the room was stifling and so dark. Although Sarah appreciated Mary's need for a change, it was another two days before she could be persuaded to bring forward the 'upsitting' time and allow Mary out of bed to sit in a chair.

The baby was to be baptised on Sunday. An hour before the service, Susanna Gurwood sent her daughters out to gather wild flowers to decorate the church. They returned with sweet peas, maiden pinks and meadowsweet. Jane Gurwood made sure the meadowsweet leaves were scattered on the floor of the nave and around the font while she arranged the flowers in vases, trusting that the heady scent would mask the dank, fusty odour of the church.

William's mother brought round the Jordan christening sheet with its lace trimmings and made William wait patiently with her outside the house. He still had not seen Mary and had another week or so to wait until she was up and about the house. Mary wrapped the baby up and pinned a tiny witch brooch into the sheet where it wouldn't be seen. She then called for Kate who handed the baby over to Elizabeth on the doorstep.

'Mind tha doesn't trail christenin' sheet i' dust,' Kate warned. 'Bairn's just 'ad a feed so 'e should sleep all through it.'

William peered across to see the baby's face; he was surprised at how small it was. He didn't know what to say and stood awkwardly with the women. Kate saw his discomfort.

'Mary's fine,' she said. 'She misses thee.'

He nodded, then turned and trailed up the lane to meet the godparents outside the church. As well as her sister, Elizabeth, Mary had chosen her brother, Matthew, and William's Uncle David to be sponsors. The bells stopped ringing just as William and the godparents walked solemnly into church, and the morning service began.

It was strange for Mary to be left alone in the house with Kate – suddenly no more fuss and excitement, and not even the baby to look after.

'Cheer up,' said Kate. 'Tha bairn must be baptised quick to save 'is soul an' tha'll soon 'ave 'im back.'

Instead of rushing off to do her jobs, she sat with Mary to keep her company. Mary ate her porridge in silence.

'William's pleased as punch wi' bairn,' Kate reported. 'I tell thee, 'e looked real proud when 'e saw 'im. Won't be long now. Tha'll see William soon. Before long tha'll be so busy tha'll wish for quiet borin' days again.'

'Maybe,' Mary answered with tears in her eyes. 'I don't know though. I miss being outside and it's been such a lovely week. I've missed hay-making.'

'There'll be others. Just thank Lord both thee an' bairn are well.'

'I know. I'm being ungrateful but I can't wait to be out and about – and be myself again.'

The baby slept right through the morning service as if drugged by his last feed. He didn't even wake when Elizabeth carried him to the font. The vicar, William and the godparents gathered in a circle. Matthew kept looking down at his boots and pushed around with his foot the meadowsweet leaves strewn over the cobbled floor. He crushed a few leaves with his toe to smell the sharp scent and braced himself as the vicar began the baptism.

'Dearly beloved, forasmuch as all men are conceived and born in sin: and that our saviour Christ saith, none can enter into the kingdom of God, except he be regenerate and born anew of water and of the Holy Ghost: I beseech you to call upon God the Father, through our Lord Jesus Christ, that of his bounteous mercy he will grant to this child that thing which by nature he cannot have; that he may be baptised with water and the Holy Ghost, and received into Christ's holy church, and be made a lively member of the same.'

Matthew was uncomfortable. The rich smell of the flowers was giving him a headache and the church was oppressive as he thought of his own lonely life. To take his mind off the vicar's words, he concentrated on one vase, thinking how funny and fluffy the flowers looked. When the vicar spoke directly to the godparents he was forced to pay more attention.

'I demand therefore, dost thou, in the name of this child, renounce the devil and all his works, the vain pomp and glory of the world, with all covetous desires of the same, and the carnal desires of the flesh, so that thou wilt not follow, nor be led by them?'

They replied, 'I renounce them all.' Matthew was sickened by it. I'm a childless widower at the age of twenty-five, he thought. I've already as good as renounced carnal desires.

The baptism continued while his thoughts were elsewhere. Thomas was duly named and the holy water sprinkled over his head without waking him. Matthew was surprised to see the baby look so lifeless in the vicar's arms; no doubt William would have preferred the boy to show more spirit. He joined half-heartedly in the mumbling of The Lord's Prayer and kept his head bowed when exhorted to make sure Thomas would learn the Christian faith. As soon as the gifts were given to William, he escaped and went home.

The others lingered awhile outside the church to take a first look at the new baby. William was proud to have a son but couldn't wait for his gander month to be over, couldn't wait to have Mary churched, and get back to their life together.

Chapter 15

Although Mary missed William and regretted not being outdoors, she began at last to appreciate her month 'in the straw'. Confined to her room for another week, she relaxed and planned the celebration feast with her sister. Over a dozen women would be invited. Along with her mother and those present at the birth, there'd be William's mother and aunts plus all William's cousins, which unfortunately included Isabella Jordan. She felt obliged to ask the eldest Gurwood girl, Jane, but then she'd have to ask William's sister, Anna. No doubt this would lead to Cecilia Gurwood, and then William's younger sister, Dorothy, would also expect to come. She decided finally that anyone under the age of fifteen was too young and reduced the number of guests to twelve.

The women without children of their own took on the task of preparing the food. Mary's sister, Elizabeth, did most of the organising and arranged things well with William's cousin, Elizabeth Cooke. The two Elizabeths were getting along fine until Isabella Jordan stepped in to help.

'Oh no,' whispered Mary's sister. 'Now you'll understand why too many cooks spoil the broth.'

Isabella tried to take control and the three of them battled it out in the kitchen. Mary could hear them crashing about and arguing, with poor Kate in the middle not knowing who to fetch things for or what to do first. Somehow, between them, they managed to produce a fruit cake and a dozen bacon and onion pasties.

On the morning of the feast the same women arrived to make oatcakes. Any one of them could have done the job perfectly but the four of them fussed and argued. They couldn't agree on the ingredients, whether to use dripping or butter, and whether to add eggs or not. As the oatcakes were for a special feast, they decided to add eggs. Isabella raised her eyebrows.

'I'm sayin' nowt. Wait till tha tries to roll it out – then tha'll know.' She watched, arms folded, as Kate mixed the oatmeal, salt and flour, and added the melted dripping, the eggs and boiling water.

'Put another egg yolk in,' ordered Elizabeth. 'It'll make it more rich.'

Isabella was not happy. She shouted at Kate. 'Yon mixture's *far* too runny. Give it 'ere. I'll sort it out.' She grabbed the basin off Kate and began to add more oatmeal. Kate grumbled under her breath and scattered oatmeal onto the table for shaping the cakes.

'Not too much,' said the Elizabeths.

'Don't listen to them two,' said Isabella. 'Put plenty on. Don't want cakes stickin' to table.'

When it came to forming the dough, Isabella was right. The mixture in Kate's hands was too soft, wet and sticky. Kate held up her hands in despair, her fingers clagged together. Elizabeth scraped the mixture off with a knife and reluctantly added more meal. When at last Kate achieved a workable dough, the four women stood round the table and glared at each other. Each one had their own opinions as to the shape and size of an oatcake. Isabella had even brought her own cutter. Kate was fed up.

'Why can't we just share it out an' make what we like,' she dared to offer. The others sighed, saw the sense in it and grabbed a handful of dough. When all the cakes had been cooked on the griddle, they stood, hands on hips, and stared at the odd assortment.

'Hmm,' commented Isabella. 'I've never seen owt so peculiar i' me life, but I reckon they'll taste all right.' With that the four cooks cleaned up the mess in sullen silence. It was just a matter now of arranging all the food on the table. Kate brought out a large cheese sent by Dorothy Jordan and set it on a plate. Mary's mother had sent some hardboiled pullet eggs and the two aunts pots of honey and rowanberry jelly.

The day of the feast was exactly two weeks after the birthing and Mary was permitted at last to leave the darkened parlour. She was so glad to be able to walk into her kitchen and wander about putting things back in their proper places. The sun shone through the window, but she was not allowed outside yet. She went back to the parlour, still curtained because of the baby, and waited for the guests to arrive.

When Kate told her it was time for the feast, Mary almost regretted inviting so many. The guests were crowded into the kitchen. They all looked genuinely pleased for her and, when her mother walked over and kissed her, Mary could have cried.

'Well done, Mary. I'm proud o' thee.' This was the cue for everyone to push forward and congratulate her on becoming a mother – all except Isabella Jordan.

'Come on, you lot,' she said. 'We want to enjoy this feast. Don't want tears dilutin' our caudle.'

'Aye. Where's caudle?' asked Dorothy Jordan. 'Let's get started.' Pots were soon filled and Elizabeth proposed a toast.

'Here's to Mary and her new bairn,' she shouted.

'To Mary an' bairn,' they echoed, and then the younger visitors threw themselves onto the food.

'Tha'd think some folks 'ad never been fed!' complained Dorothy. She and the other older women held off politely. They gathered in a corner of the room and whispered critical comments about the pile of oatcakes.

'Never seen owt like it. 'Ow can tha go wrong wi' oatcakes?'

'Never in all my puff 'ave I seen one *that* shape an' size!'

Dorothy went to pick one out. 'This one's enough to break tha teeth on,' she said. 'I'll try suckin' it.'

'Dip it i' caudle,' Sarah Ezard suggested. 'That'll soften it up a bit.'

As Dorothy left her oatcake to soak, she colluded with Sarah on the youngsters' dresses and the way they'd tied their hair. She then peered round the kitchen looking to find fault with Mary's arrangements. There'd be plenty of time to put her straight. After a while, feeling they were left out, she and the other elders said their polite goodbyes.

Once the youngsters realised they were on their own they relaxed and began to gossip. Isabella's sister, Susan, piped up.

'Tell us, Elizabeth. Is it true what they say about Robert's rod?'

'Susan! Shush,' interrupted Isabella. 'Thoo's not even courtin' yet. Thoo shouldn't know about such things.'

'Is it though? Is it true?'

'Yes, Elizabeth,' the others joined in, 'we'd all like to know.'

'Well ...' said Elizabeth. 'It depends on the weather.' And they all laughed. Elizabeth blushed and added, 'I'm not saying anymore. It's between him and me.'

''Ardly *between*! *In* more like, eh?' Susan sniggered and everyone burst out laughing again.

'You've been drinking too much caudle,' said Elizabeth.

Susan held a hand to her mouth and giggled. Even her sister, Isabella, was beginning to unwind a little, glad to be out of the house and free of responsibilities for a change. Kate recognised this and went to refill Isabella's mug and offer her more pasties.

The two Gurwood girls sat side by side like statues on the settle with William's sister Anna, wary of joining in.

'Come on, you three,' cajoled Mary, 'have some more cheese and fruit cake. There's plenty.' Shyly, they helped themselves.

Jane Gurwood looked rather flushed and bright-eyed. As Mary watched the Gurwood sisters she reflected, not for the first time, on how attractive the eldest sister was – by far the prettiest. The others, all seven of them, were like peas in a pod, all having straight brown hair like their mother and dark, beady eyes. Jane, however, took after her father. She had striking blue eyes and her hair was wavy, almost black. The vicar often boasted that Jane's hair was as 'shiny as the best carriage horse.' Yet Mary was sorry for her. Jane's mother had been pregnant every two years and Jane had been forced to act like a second mother with so many sisters to look after. As if reading Mary's thoughts, Jane looked up from her plate.

'Don't be like my mother,' she said, 'and have just the one baby boy and then nothing but girls.'

Susan wiped crumbs from her mouth and put her hand up to speak. 'I think there must be summat i' water tha father drinks,' she said. 'Which well does tha use?'

'Knox Well, of course,' said Jane. 'It's the nearest.'

'Can't be that,' thought Mary aloud, 'because Jordans use that too and they have plenty of sons.'

'Must be way men does it then.'

'Susan!' shouted Mary. 'You're too young to have such ideas.'

'I 'eard Dickon i' stable tellin' Tom that it sometimes was that way wi' 'orses.'

'What? Horses can only do it one way. What *are* you talking about?'

'Don't know then.' Susan was out of her depth and wished she'd not brought up the subject.

Jane Gurwood looked pensive. 'It could be connected with what the father eats,' she wondered. 'My father eats a lot of cheese and milky porridge. Maybe if he ate more meat he'd have sons.'

'I've 'eard it takes a real man to make lasses,' Susan butted in again. 'So tha father must be somethin' special. A real stud!'

That shocked them – the thought of a well-endowed vicar.

Mary was amazed at Susan. 'You seem to know a lot about such things,' she said. 'I think we'd better make sure your brothers keep an eye on you.'

'I bet it's her brothers she's getting all this from,' Elizabeth decided. 'I bet it's Leeman, isn't it?'

'Well, I've got to learn some time.' That ended the conversation. Susan finished her drink in one go and refilled the pot.

As they drank more caudle they became sleepy and sentimental. Jane suggested they sang a few songs before going home. She started them off and they sat in a circle, arm in arm, swaying to the rhythm of a well-known ballad about young love.

Mary leant back in her chair, happy but quite exhausted. She was relieved when they all left and she was alone again with just Kate and the baby. Tomorrow, William would be allowed to visit.

Chapter 16

All week William had been so restless that, on the day of Mary's feast, his father pulled him aside before breakfast. He rested his hands on William's shoulders and looked him straight in the eye.

'There's 'orse all saddled up an' ready. Get thassen off to 'Unmanby market an' buy summat for Mary. Thoo's a waste o' space 'ere – like a cat on an 'ot 'earth.'

William was grateful for this unexpected change in routine and made his way westwards along the dewy tracks to Hunmanby. As the sun rose higher above the sea and began to warm his back, he thought of Mary. Tomorrow he could be alone with her. The prospect took his breath away.

When he reached the market it was already full of people. After leaving his horse behind The White Swan, he wandered from stall to stall, side-stepping the baskets and sheets laid out on the ground. He soon became hot and confused in the noisy crowd. Folk shouted in his ear and grabbed his arm as he passed, so eager were they to sell their wares. He'd forgotten how cramped the market place could get and wasn't sure what Mary would like. Would beads or ribbons do, or maybe a length of material for a new gown?

To give himself time to think, he sat outside the inn in the sunshine and drank a mug of ale. Nothing sprang to mind. He watched dejectedly as a group of women walked past swapping recipes as they went. It gave him an idea.

When he left the inn he traipsed up and down again, this time looking at all the edibles on display. He soon lost heart again and would have gone home empty-handed if a young woman sitting on the roadside hadn't pulled at his leg. She soon persuaded him to buy some raisins and a pot of treacle. Pleased with himself, he set off for home as fast as he could so as not to miss too much of the day's work.

The ride was refreshing. The sun was well up by now and a cool breeze was blowing in from the sea. The white cliffs of Bempton shone in the distance and the ripening corn was golden under the blue sky. By the time he reached Reighton, he was more relaxed than he'd been in days.

The next morning, Mary sat in the parlour waiting for William's visit. She drummed her fingers on the small table and couldn't keep her feet still. Although eager to see him again, she envied his freedom and couldn't help feeling cheated. She'd missed out on the hay-making and would probably not be at the harvest. When she heard him knock, her heart leapt. With mixed emotions she went to the door. She was desperate to hug him and be held close but, instead, she led him into the kitchen to sit and have a drink and share some curd cheesecake.

He sat stiffly on the bench and looked as if he was new to the house. To William, the place smelled of women and babies. He'd built it but didn't feel he belonged there anymore. He resented the month of confinement that had driven him away. Mary took his hand across the table and squeezed it. He looked up into her face and experienced the familiar lurch in his stomach.

'How long now?' he asked hoarsely.

'Just another week indoors, then I can sit out in the garden. I can do little jobs now. I won't be so bored. I can't wait to be outside again.'

'And then ... churching. And then ... *I* come back home.'

'Yes,' she added with a blush. 'I'm quite well, I think. But you know ...' Neither could voice their fears that it might take some time to get back to their old ways in bed together. To mask their embarrassment William asked to see the baby. When he held him he marvelled at the light weight and peered at his face to see who he was like. Something about the eyebrows reminded him of Mary's father.

'What have you got in your bag?' Mary asked.

'Oh, I was forgetting. I've brought you something from Hunmanby.' He returned the baby carefully to the crib and took out the packet of raisins and pot of treacle.

Mary was disappointed. She'd have preferred something more personal, something of no obvious use. Still, it was the thought that counted.

'Oh, you shouldn't have. Thank you. I'll make a special pudding when you come back home and I'll save some raisins for winter.'

'I thought … what with you always inventing new recipes and all.'

'Mmm.' The conversation petered out. They behaved like strangers.

When he left, he gave her a quick, almost brotherly kiss on the cheek. He ached inside as he walked up the steep hill back to Uphall.

After almost four weeks of confinement, Mary prepared to be churched. She could once again be part of the community and William would return home with her after the service. George Gurwood suggested she bring the baby along. She could leave after the brief ceremony or choose to stay and listen to his sermon if the baby was asleep.

Mary spent most of the morning with Kate deciding what to wear. She chose her best linen gown and petticoat but couldn't decide on the hat – whether to wear the felt one that matched her blue gown or the more fashionable straw one. As the weather was sunny she chose the straw hat, changed its ribbons to blue and picked out a pretty Irish linen wrap for her shoulders.

Kate smiled but envied her the choice of clothes. 'Thoo looks good enough to eat.'

Mary smiled. 'Thanks,' she said, 'but will the petticoat hang well when I've got my pattens on?' She fastened them on and clattered round the parlour.

'There's no real difference,' Kate offered, 'an' anyways tha can leave 'em outside church.'

'Right, I think I'm ready then. What about Thomas? Is everything clean? I saw his bonnet on the floor yesterday – that won't do it any good.'

'Don't fret, I've washed it since. Sit thassen down an' rest. It'll be all right. Feed Thomas an' just … rest!'

This was easier said than done. Mary was on tenterhooks because William would be back home today. It seemed ages since they'd been properly alone together, much longer than four weeks. She stood chewing her nails and wandered over to the window to pull the curtain back and peer out. Kate tapped her on the shoulder. She'd carried Thomas over to be fed.

This was another thing that was making Mary nervous. Thomas wasn't feeding as he should or gaining weight. Either he didn't have the strength to suck properly or else there just wasn't enough milk there. Sarah had said they might give him butter from a cow that had eaten butterwort. Failing that they could try diluted cow's or goat's milk, or maybe find a wet nurse. Susanna Gurwood was still breastfeeding her latest daughter, but Mary thought it improper to ask a vicar's wife. She looked down at Thomas who was already falling asleep again after only sucking for a minute or two.

'It's no good, Kate. I keep pinching him, but he won't wake and feed.'

'When thoo's more settled, then 'e might perk up. Maybe all 'e needs is some fresh air.'

'That's what I need! I can't wait to be walking about and getting on with my jobs like everyone else.' She looked down again at Thomas. 'And you, young man, had better think on. You don't take after your father. He'd have drunk all the milk offered, he would.' She snuggled and kissed him before wrapping him up again.

It was bright and sunny as Mary and Kate set off for church with the baby. On the way they called at Sarah Ezard's for reassurance. There was something about Sarah that made Mary feel protected and sheltered in a way she'd never felt with her own mother.

''Ow's bairn comin' on?' Sarah asked. 'Feedin' any better?'

'Not really.'

'Don't worry. We'll soon 'ave 'im sorted. Give it time. Come in for a moment so I can see 'im.' Once they were in the dark kitchen, she pulled aside the veil from the baby's eyes. She thought he looked pale and sickly. ''E's what I call an angel baby. 'E still thinks 'e's in 'eaven and doesn't know 'e 'as to start livin'. 'E'll soon catch on. Won't be long before 'e realises 'ow 'ungry 'e is.'

Mary hoped so.

As she walked further up the hill, she met others on their way to church. Everyone appeared pleased to see her out again. When she turned to enter the churchyard, she glanced at the Filey cliffs under the blue sky, looking so close she could almost reach out and touch them. She could see the waves splashing over the Brigg. As clouds passed over the sun, the ravines in the cliffs changed colour from the pale purple of dry heather to a leaden blue then to a rich bracken-brown. She breathed in deeply, relishing the sea air and realised how much she'd missed this view.

With some reluctance she entered the dim church and seated herself with Kate and the baby at the back beside the font, apart from the rest of the congregation. She was quite aware that many still thought women were unclean until churched. George Gurwood did his best to lighten the purification service and make it into a true thanksgiving. He smiled and signalled to Mary to come and kneel at the altar. She lowered her eyes and gazed at the green carpet as he began.

'Forasmuch as it hath pleased Almighty God of his goodness to give you safe deliverance, and hath preserved you in the great danger of child-birth: you shall therefore give hearty thanks unto God, and say I am well pleased: that the Lord hath heard the voice of my prayer ... The snares of death compassed me round about: and the pains of hell gat hold of me. I found trouble and heaviness, and I called upon the name of the Lord ... I was in misery, and he helped me ... Glory be to the Father, and to the Son and to the Holy Ghost; as it was in the beginning, is now, and ever shall be: world without end. Amen.'

Mary joined in when they said The Lord's Prayer. She heard Ben's voice above the others and could also pick out William's. After brief exhortations and responses came the final prayer.

'O Almighty God, we give thee humble thanks for thou hast vouchsafed to deliver this woman thy servant from the great pain and peril of child-birth.' The vicar then asked Mary to follow God's will faithfully in her present life and partake of everlasting glory in the life to come. And that was that. She was churched.

The Gurwood girls gave identical smiles as she walked past them to collect her baby. Then she joined William sitting in the Jordan pew. Her sister, Elizabeth, winked at her from the other side of the nave. Her brother managed a smile. William took Mary's hand in his and gave it a little squeeze. She was part of the real world again and was loved and respected. She'd not realised before how becoming a mother was such an important rite of passage. She looked up at the altar and swallowed hard, relieved that it had all gone so well.

Chapter 17

After church, Mary and William ate dinner at Uphall with the Jordan family and left as soon as they could. Kate was away for the rest of the day visiting her mother and they'd have the house to themselves. However, once alone in the kitchen, Mary fussed round rearranging things she'd already put away while William fidgeted and hovered about with nothing to do. The fine warm weather gave Mary an idea.

'Why don't we sit in the garden until Thomas has another feed?'

So William sat on the chopping log and lit up his pipe and Mary brought out a stool. She settled herself down by the open door so she could listen for the baby. She also brought out her knitting to keep her hands busy. They sat without talking for quite a while, listening to the birds and the distant bleating of sheep on the moor. The giant dock leaves at the edge of the garden were now a deep red and had gone to seed. Plenty of small apples studded the tree and everything in the garden looked peaceful. The clicking of Mary's needles slowed to a gentler rhythm and at last William began to talk quietly about his stay at Uphall, the state of the barley and who had not kept the hedges in good repair.

'You know it's taken me a month at Uphall to see just how annoying Francis can be. Poor Anna has to keep the peace.'

'But she's only sixteen.'

'Maybe, but she's an old head on her.'

'It's probably because she's had to look after all your younger brothers and sisters,' Mary offered.

'And guess who's mother's favourite?'

'Is it you?' Mary wouldn't have been surprised.

'I wish it was. No – it's the youngest, Richard. He's just two. Mother says she's not having any more children.'

'She's been saying that for years.'

'You know I was just thinking the other day, my parents have added nine Jordans to the village. And now we've just added another one. That's a lot of Jordans.' He smiled, leant back against the wall and puffed gently on his pipe. 'The Smiths on the other hand,' he continued, 'are not doing half as well. Your sister's been married for well over a year now and still has no child. And poor Matthew – he's a widower with no issue.'

Mary shivered and dropped a stitch. It was like tempting fate. The tide had turned and the wind was now coming in off the sea, bringing with it a light mist.

'It's suddenly gone cold,' she said. 'Shall we go in?'

William stood up and stretched and knocked out his pipe against the log. 'Aye, best get in. You don't want to catch cold. I think I'll just wander over to Ben's while you feed Thomas. I want to see how his bees are doing.'

She was disappointed that he didn't want to keep her company while she fed the baby. It would have been pleasant. Instead, she fed the baby alone in the darkened parlour and wondered how long William would be.

Ben was surprised to see William and made no bones about telling him what he thought about a young husband leaving his wife on a Sunday.

'Bees'll be 'ere when we're not,' he said. 'Get thassen back 'ome to Mary where tha belongs. Don't think tha can come waddlin' over 'ere any time tha feels left out.' As William left Ben's, he was handed a pot of honey. 'An' that's for Mary an' young bairn. Not for a great swill-kite like thee.'

Mary had time to think while she fed the baby. She decided she'd be more open and loving towards William and see if that had any effect. So, when he walked in the door holding out the honey, she jumped up and put her arms round him. She pressed her warm breasts against his chest and, sure enough, he bent his head to kiss her on the lips. Holding her tightly in return, he whispered in her ear.

'Is it all right yet? I mean, are you well enough after having Thomas?'

'I don't know. I suppose we could try – as long as you're careful.'

They retired early that night and, since it was such a warm evening, took off all their clothes. Mary got into bed first and lay under the light coverlet praying the baby wouldn't wake up and spoil everything. William looked very handsome in the candlelight as he strolled naked towards the bed, his body ready for action. As he climbed in beside her, already breathing fast, she warned him.

'Go steady, will you? Pretend I'm a virgin.'

'Now don't get me over-excited. I'll have enough trouble trying to go gently.' He leant on one elbow and began to kiss her. She soon responded and, when he rolled on top, realised just how much she'd missed him. As slowly as he could he eased himself inside. She appreciated his thoughtfulness but could not relax, still fearful of some damage it might do. Also her nipples were tender and she was conscious of her breasts growing heavy with milk. William carried on his lovemaking, not thrusting too much though she guessed it went against all his instincts. It was soon over and he slid out and lay on his back.

'Well,' he sighed with a smile, 'that wasn't easy. I wanted to push in further.'

'It was all right for you though?'

'Oh yes. I'm not complaining.'

'We'll soon be back to normal, you'll see.' She turned towards him and kissed him before snuggling up against his damp chest. A familiar aroma of tobacco hung round them as she fell asleep in his arms.

By mid-August they were themselves again, the harvest was in full swing and the weather was favourable for a second hay-making. The only problem was baby Thomas. William's young sister, Anna, came round one day and gave Mary a shock.

'I heard your milk turns sour if you sleep with your husband when you're feeding a baby.'

Mary stopped what she was doing. 'Who told you that?' she demanded.

'Francis.'

'I might have known.'

'He says it's the man's juice that does it. It curdles your milk.'

'Well I've never heard of it. Sarah never said anything. It can't be true. We'd all know such things. Why half the village wouldn't have survived if that's what happens. Look at Susanna Gurwood – you can't tell me George doesn't – oh, I don't know why I'm even talking to you like this. Francis shouldn't tell you such stuff. I'm going to have words with your mother.'

'No. Don't do that. He'll only take it out on me. You don't know what he's like.'

'No, but I'm beginning to get an inkling.'

When Anna had gone Mary wondered if there might be some truth in it. Who was to know? Dare she ask William? It would spoil things between them and then he'd be distant again. In the end she asked her sister Elizabeth to find out.

'It's an old wives' tale,' Elizabeth reported back. 'I didn't dare ask the vicar's wife but I'm sure George and Susanna never worry about such things.'

In the end it didn't matter what milk Thomas drank – most or all of it came back up. Mary tried various remedies. She drank milkwort tea in an effort to increase the flow of her milk, but Thomas never wanted much anyway. Sarah suggested she bathe her breasts in hot then cold water. She told her never to stand too long with her hands in liquids and avoid strenuous jobs. Nothing helped, and Thomas was languishing.

'Oh why can't you keep your milk down?' Mary cried. Her nipples were sore from the constant attempts to feed him and both she and Kate were fed up with the rich smell of his linen whenever they changed him. He'd look as if he was hungry but then resist her and not take a full hold or suck properly. She'd be gentle and coaxing at first, stroking his cheek and lips with her finger but then, after failing to tempt him, she'd shout.

'Oh, Thomas! For pity's sake, drink! I'm sick to death of you messing about.' Even when he did manage to drink, she was sure he'd puke it up again. The only mystery was when it would happen – it was quite unpredictable. William almost ran out of the room the first time he saw the milk shoot out.

'We won't be able to have visitors,' he complained. 'You can't have folk sitting in their best clothes and having to face that … that mess. There's no knowing when he's going to do it. I've not seen anything like it.' Mary's eyes filled with tears. Thomas was making her feel like an outcast.

Kate stood by her, forever optimistic. 'Sarah says some bairns are like this till they get walkin', an' then they're all right.'

But, thought Mary, he'll not reach the age of walking if he doesn't feed. She couldn't afford a full-time wet nurse to live in and neither she nor William wanted that; they feared that babies took on the character of whoever nursed them. If anyone else was going to feed Thomas it would have to be someone they respected and knew well. It was Sarah who eventually persuaded Mary to go and see the vicar's wife.

Susanna Gurwood was only too happy to help. She had ample milk and was genuinely concerned about Thomas. However, she hadn't reckoned on the frustration and anxiety he'd give. He'd start to drink as if hungry and then cry out in pain. He fidgeted and then, if he did manage to drink, Susanna would soon see her milk disgorged again – either in his crib or down her apron. She tried keeping him upright after what seemed a successful feed and she, Mary and Kate took turns in pacing the room with him. Soon the whole village knew about the troubles with Thomas and many shook their heads.

''E'll not be long for this world. I've seen it before,' Martha Wrench told the other wives. 'Sarah's done 'er best.

There's nowt for it but prayer. It's i' God's 'ands now, poor bairn.'

Thomas began to develop other symptoms, some of them quite frightening. He wheezed and coughed and his cry became hoarse and pitiful. Sometimes his vomit was streaked with blood and there were moments when Mary thought he'd stopped breathing. At such times her heart raced and in panic she'd call for Kate or William.

One morning in September, Mary woke early and went straight to the crib as usual. In the semi-darkness she leant over and peered inside. Thomas looked peaceful in his sleep but she couldn't tell whether he was breathing or not. She brushed his face with a finger and leapt back. His cheek was cold as ice. Her heart pounding, she grabbed him and lifted him out. His head lolled as she shook him and tried to wake him, but it was no use. With a gasp she almost threw him back into the crib and stared wide-eyed at the small lifeless body. Her knees buckled and she collapsed onto the floor, one hand over her mouth and the other shaking as it clutched the crib.

William found Mary an hour later, still kneeling on the floor. There was no fire lit and no breakfast ready. He rested his arm on her shoulder and looked into the crib. It was as he'd feared.

'It's not your fault,' he whispered. 'We should've expected it. Don't be too upset – these things happen. The baby was never meant to be.'

She shrugged his arm away and began to cry.

'You'll have other children,' he added.

'I don't *want* other children,' she shouted, her throat choked. 'I want little Thomas.'

He ignored her and went to see to his own breakfast. When he left the house she was still on the floor, twisting her hands in and out of each other as if she didn't know what to do with them.

Kate went to help as soon as William told her the news. She took the baby and washed him and wrapped him in a clean sheet. Mary looked on, helpless. Kate made some porridge for them both and wondered how long she dared stay.

'Mary,' she said, 'I'll have to be gettin' back to Up'all. They're still busy with 'arvest. I'll come again later.' Mary hardly heard her.

As it was one of the busiest times of the year, William was out of the house from dawn till dusk. Mary sat by the window, constantly close to tears and wanting him back home. Afraid of losing her mind, she just wanted to be hugged and held close. Sometimes she thought she was held together by nothing more substantial than soft, unspun wool. Kate did a great job making sure that meals were ready on time, and Sarah and Elizabeth came every day to see if Mary was all right. Without them she knew she'd be lost. William did not come home until it was almost too dark to see, and hardly had time to eat his supper before falling asleep. Next to him in bed, listening to his snores, Mary lay wide awake and stared into the darkness.

The funeral took place a few days after Thomas's death and was a quiet and brief affair. Not many attended since most were out in the field or back in their yards helping with the harvest. Elizabeth and Matthew came with their mother and also William's uncle and aunt. That was all. The Jordans at Uphall said they couldn't be spared at harvest time and yet, when the field workers heard the bell tolling for the funeral, they all stopped work and were silent. The men doffed their hats in respect. Death at reaping time was particularly hard. They each had their own thoughts on mortality as they began again to scythe down the barley. Some of the older men swung with more vigour as if to affirm their health and strength.

As the bells ceased tolling, George Gurwood led the small group through the churchyard to the north east corner where a tiny grave lay open. William carried Thomas in the children's coffin.

George Gurwood stood by his side and recited, 'I am the resurrection and the life, saith the Lord: he that believeth in me, though he were dead, yet shall he live.'

Mary clenched her fists when he reached the part 'And though, after my skin, worms destroy this body.' She couldn't bear to think of leaving Thomas alone in the dark, damp soil to be eaten away. She looked to the sky for help, tears pouring from her screwed up eyes. George Gurwood was relentless.

'The Lord gave, and the Lord hath taken away; blessed be the name of the Lord.' He deemed it inappropriate to read the customary Bible readings so indicated that they should now take the baby from the coffin and lay him in the ground. Mary watched through blurred eyes as the tiny knotted shroud was lowered in.

'Forasmuch as it hath pleased Almighty God of his great mercy to take unto himself the soul of our dear brother here departed, we therefore commit his body to the ground; earth to earth, ashes to ashes, dust to dust.'

Elizabeth gave Mary a gentle nudge to remind her of the flowers in their hands. Together they dropped them into the hole – a small crown of daisies from Elizabeth and a bunch of wild white roses from Mary. William bent down and grabbed a handful of the freshly dug earth and let it fall on his son. The last prayers were said, and they walked away leaving the sexton to fill in the grave.

Chapter 18

No one stayed long at the funeral feast though Kate had prepared plenty of cold ham, pickles and ale. Everyone had work to do. Mary and Kate were soon left alone to tidy up in the now silent house. Mary's breasts were still tender and she kept looking towards the empty crib. Suddenly she told Kate to stick the crib up in the loft. She was sick of the sight of it.

William was relieved to get outside and return to the harvesting. He stood at the edge of the field and gazed around. The barley was almost all mown, and the men were gathering with their dogs ready to kill any rabbits hidden in the remaining stalks. He recalled the young rabbit he'd killed last harvest, the startled innocence in its eyes. He'd seen it then as a bad omen. Now he connected it with the death of his son who hadn't had much chance either, cut down before his life had really begun.

Words from the Bible reverberated in his head and unnerved him – 'whatever a man soweth, that shall he also reap.' He knew he'd been over-proud of having a son. 'Pride goeth before destruction and an haughty spirit before a fall.'

He kept his guilt to himself, unable to confide in anyone, least of all his wife.

Mary had plenty of time to reflect on her year so far. God had been cruel to her. The loss of Thomas was enough to cope with, but she'd missed out on the hay-making and also the harvest. Now it was late October and the weather was cold, autumnal and wet. She felt cheated stuck indoors yet again, especially as she was now alone and with no baby to look after.

By November, she realised she was with child again. Although pleased to be given another chance, this time she had morning sickness. There were many under-the-breath mutterings from Dorothy Jordan and the older generation; everyone had their own ideas about the sex of the coming baby. On one of her rare visits to the house down St. Helen's Lane, Dorothy interrogated Mary.

'Does tha crave for sweet stuff? Does tha feel moody? Let's look at thee.' She pulled some strands of hair from under Mary's cap. 'I wonder, is it duller an' thinner?' Mary pushed her hair back in. 'Is tha water a dull yellow i' mornin'?'

Mary wondered if Dorothy cared for her at all, or was only interested in her for breeding purposes, like a stock cow.

'Get Sarah to come an' dangle yon weddin' ring over tha belly. Then we'll see. I reckon it'll be a lass thoo's 'avin'.'

'It's true,' said Mary. 'I do want sugary things. I don't know about the moody part but I could check my water.'

'Aye, an' fetch Sarah, like I said.' Then, without even sitting down or asking about William, she went to the door to let herself out. With her hand on the latch she called back. 'Mind thoo drinks a good draught o' sage ale every mornin'. Don't forget. I'll get Martha Wrench to make sure she's got plenty brewin'. Well, I'll be off then.'

She went out before Mary could ask after her family at Uphall. Sometimes Mary thought she'd never be close to her mother-in-law. There was something hard and unforgiving in the woman. Maybe it was living with so many men and hired hands; all compassion had been knocked out of her.

For much of that autumn Mary was low in spirits and only went through the motions of her daily chores. She couldn't shake off her sadness and guilt about baby Thomas and now, on top of it all, she was nauseous. Baking bread was the worst time; the smell of a fresh yeasty loaf made her retch. She'd been fine while pregnant before. Maybe the old wives' tales were true. All the queasiness might mean she was having a girl.

Kate was a godsend. Early each morning she milked the cows in the pasture, and again in the afternoon. Till now she'd sold any surplus milk to others or exchanged it for vegetables. She now pestered Mary about the need to use the milkhouse properly. It had been a wasted space so far and she was keen to get the room organised.

It was just the distraction Mary needed. They spent a full day together washing the walls and sweeping and cleaning the floor. One day Kate went round the village and managed to get an old wooden churn, a plunger and a pair of butter spades. After scrubbing them clean she brought in a large shallow pancheon from the kitchen, poured fresh milk into it and then left it overnight to settle.

Next morning Kate and Mary skimmed off the raft of cream with ladles and poured it into the churn. Then they took turns to work the churn staff up and down. If it hadn't been for Kate, Mary would have given up. It seemed to take forever. The steady rhythm of the plunger was giving her a headache and she began to feel dizzy. Kate saw that Mary was looking flushed.

'Maybe tha shouldn't do so much when wi' child. Let me finish off,' she suggested. Mary sat down on a stool, wiped her forehead and put her head between her knees. She'd only been churning for about ten minutes. Kate told her to listen out for the change in noise, for the thick slushing to grow muffled as the curds separated out. After another ten minutes the churn sounded loud and hollow and Kate stopped.

'If I overdoes it,' she explained, 'butter'll taste too strong.' She pulled out the plunger and poured everything onto a piece of muslin stretched over a bucket. Mary had never shown any interest in such tasks as a child, much to her mother's dismay. Now she followed Kate's every move and listened attentively to her instructions. Kate explained how the churn had separated the curds from the buttermilk. Now the liquid was straining through the sieve. Mary watched her tie the curds up in the muslin and squeeze out some last drops. Kate gestured towards the bucket with her head.

'Save that for drinkin' or we can make scones or pancakes with it. It makes good porridge an' all.' She held up the bag of curds. 'Look 'ere, butter's already takin' shape. I'll wash it to get rid of any buttermilk or it'll taste rancid.' She washed the butter twice in clear cold water and then pressed it between two boards before finally tipping the butter out onto a cold slab. Mary saw how Kate squeezed it and kneaded it to remove any lingering buttermilk.

'The more I work it,' Kate explained patiently, 'the softer it'll be but it mustn't get over dry or it'll crumble. I want it moist like a fine mornin' dew, but firm to touch.'

Mary sighed. 'I'd no idea butter was so difficult to make.'

'It i'n't. Not if tha knows what tha's doin'.' Next, Kate took some salt from the salt box, put it in a pan of water and told Mary to boil it up really fast till all the water had gone. 'Dissolve it well first, or butter won't be an even colour.'

Mary did as she was told and returned after a few minutes. 'Look – the water's all gone,' she said. 'The salt's in lovely fine pieces now.'

Kate sprinkled it on the butter and mixed it in lightly. Then she couldn't resist showing off her skill with the butter spades. Mary watched in awe as Kate produced, in quick succession, three beautiful but very pale blocks.

'There!' Kate said with a satisfied grin. 'That's that! Tha can put 'em in a stone jar to keep.' Mary was so pleased with the results she clapped her hands together and gave Kate a kiss. There was only one disappointment.

'I did think the butter would be more yellow,' she confessed.

'Yellow? Not i' winter. Nay – what we 'ave is best butter for oatcakes an' pastry makin'. It'll stay cool an' make lovely flaky pastry. Thoo'll see.' Mary hoped Kate was right. 'Wait till we make cheese,' said Kate with a wink. 'Then tha'll know tha's got a milk'ouse! Why not get William to carve an M on yon butter spades?'

Mary smiled but was close to tears. Kate nudged her with her elbow.

'I bet tha must be carryin' a lass by looks of it. Thoo's as soft as butter these days.'

That evening William tasted his first home-made butter. It wasn't as good as that made at Uphall but he kept quiet – Mary was obviously delighted with her work.

'I'll get Kate to show me cheese-making next summer,' she said.

He grinned. 'I know where this is going to lead. You'll be experimenting with all sorts of flavours and I'll have to be the first to taste them.' He was just relieved that she looked happy again and was looking forward to the future.

Chapter 19

1706

After a hard winter, spring arrived quite suddenly. There was sleet and snow one day and the next morning a bright blue sky and warm wind blowing through the village. When this mild weather continued everyone became busy. The men were either in the fields harrowing and sowing or were at home dealing with newborn piglets and calves. Shepherds worked all hours with the lambing, and William and Dickon took advantage of the fine weather to spend days on end ploughing the Jordan land that had lain fallow. It was back-breaking work. Every night William collapsed into bed exhausted. He'd lie, not moving at all, and relax only when his aching muscles stopped twitching. Mary would nestle up to him, soft and warm, and he'd fall asleep while she talked in the dark about more plans for the garden.

One morning Mary responded to the spring sunshine and left the doors wide open. Over the winter the house had built up the distinct smells of burnt fat and smoke, and she now wanted fresh air to waft through the rooms. Kate had the idea of picking violets to perfume the house. When the two women set off, they came across Sarah Ezard bent almost double as she looked among the hedgerows. Her head was down and, so intent was she on seeking the plants she needed, she didn't even hear their greeting. When they returned home, Mary scattered petals over the parlour floor. Now the house had the scent of spring.

After Kate had gone to milk the cows, Mary decided to sit out in the garden for a while and just enjoy the weather. She took a stool from the milkhouse and sat under the apple tree. A robin was perched at the top and sang loudly. It reminded her of last spring when she was pregnant with little Thomas, when she was so full of hope. As she watched, the robin puffed out its chest and trilled some high notes. She was no longer sick in the mornings and, despite her fears, began to feel some excitement at the prospect of another child. The robin stopped singing as a gentle rain began to fall. Not wanting to go back indoors, she moved her stool under the eaves and listened to the raindrops falling on the thatch. With her head leaning against the wall, she gazed at the hawthorn leaves, freshly out of bud and a vivid green. She heard the new lambs bleating on the moor. Everything around was thriving and so alive. As if on cue, her stomach rippled like a wave as the baby turned over. She stood up and walked into the rain, lifting her face up to the drops, full of hope once more.

William was also appreciating the spring. He trudged back down the hill after ploughing all day and, although his back ached, he was aware of the thatched roofs glowing pink in the sunset. The loud singing of the birds lifted his spirits. Sunsets had always inspired him; they were mellow, dreaming times when he could imagine what might be, when the day was done and the future full of hope.

William's father, also affected by the sudden change in the weather, was making plans. The poor rainfall of the last year had made him wonder about having a water cistern put in at Uphall. No one else in Reighton had one. Dickon was not impressed and grumbled about his master's plans to Tom.

'Why, we've always managed wi' wells before. Seems to me like a lot o' work for nowt. Just like Francis to try summat new.' Yet he had to admit that the wells had almost run dry last summer.

Francis Jordan decided to have the cistern built underground in one of the barns, and the deeper the better. He managed to convince Dickon by arguing on behalf of the animals.

'Our stock'll never be thirsty, see. They'll 'ave cool water i' summer an' warm water i' winter.' He calculated that a nine-foot cube would hold ninety hogsheads of water and wanted work to begin straight away on digging the hole. Since there were no free hands at the time, this first task lasted well into summer.

By the end of June there was a large, and potentially dangerous, hole in the barn. Old Ben came to look at it, stood there wondering, then went away shaking his head. Others did the same. Only William and his brothers were confident of its success but were ashamed by the slow progress. The three older brothers had hoped to just supervise the next step of plastering the sides of the hole with clay but they ended up down in the pit themselves with a trowel each. Their father stood on the edge of the great hole and shouted down at them.

'I want clay two inches thick – nowt less.' They sighed, but at least they hadn't been made to trample the clay and fetch it. At the end of the day they emerged from the depths, their shirts and breeches caked in mud. Their father showed no sympathy.

'Tha looks as if tha's all fallen down cliffs. Tomorrow tha'll 'ave to get more clay as I want bottom o' yon pit bedded out with a thicker layer.'

They wondered why they'd been so keen on this cistern in the first place. To their dismay, their father demanded that the bottom be beaten until it was smooth and even; he wanted it to feel like wax. After another gruelling day with clay up to their elbows, the cistern was almost complete. They hoped it would be worth the effort.

Kate and Mary were just as busy. In early summer Kate gathered together, as promised, the items needed for cheese-making – a shallow tub, some cheesecloth, moulds and a cheese press. She already had a scalding tub for cleaning the utensils and was determined that the milkhouse be kept spotless from now on. No one but she and Mary were to be allowed in and even they had to make sure their shoes were clean. Kate was insistent that any dirt even near the milk would ruin the taste of the butter and cheese.

'Tha's well-suited to this work,' she told Mary with a cheeky smile.

'Why?'

''Cos tha's 'avin' a bairn. No bleedin' once a month like me. Didn't tha know – cheese won't set properly wi' women at that time o' month.' Now Mary knew why her mother sometimes took over from her maid.

One morning Kate told her that some calves had been lost at Uphall and there was fresh rennet.

'If tha likes,' she said, 'we can put our clean aprons on an' get started. We musn't 'ave any interruptions an' we must take our time. Everythin's been scalded clean.' They stepped down into the white-walled room, tying on their aprons as they went. Mary shivered in the cooler air as Kate lifted the lid off a large pan.

'I've already put rennet in. I did it first thing this mornin' while milk was still warm.' Mary peered into the pan. 'Milk's already clabbered. Look there – see curds formin'? I thought we'd make a soft cheese. It's easiest an' quickest. Curds can be i' larger chunks i' soft cheeses.' Kate bent down and washed her hands in a bucket of hot water. Then she put her finger in the soft, white mess.

'I'm testin' it to see if it splits nicely when I lift me finger out.' The white curd came away cleanly and the clear whey liquid puddled into the hole left by her finger. 'Aye, it's ready. Pass me yon knife. I'm goin' to cut curds this way,' she said as she sliced vertically through the curds, 'and then I'm cuttin' 'em this way.' She sliced them into cubes. Then she put her whole hand into the pan and stirred the curds around. ''Elp me ladle out whey, then we'll strain curds.'

Once they'd got as much whey out as they could, Kate put a clean cloth over a large basin and tipped in the curds. She showed Mary how to tie the cloth into a bundle by winding one corner round the other three. Then she put the bundle on the draining board.

'We'll leave it for a while,' she said. 'Let's go an' sit i' garden for a bit.'

Mary sat on the chopping log and stretched out her legs, leaning back against the wall. She shut her eyes and held her head up to feel the warmth of the sun. Her hands rested over her tight, swollen belly.

Kate had brought out some knitting and sat down next to Mary on the milking stool. 'I mustn't waste time,' she said. 'Devil finds work for idle 'ands.'

Mary sighed. 'Don't you start,' she murmured lazily, still with her eyes shut. 'William's mother's always on to me about doing this and doing that. I'm busy enough with the garden, and making and mending clothes, and cooking and cleaning. What more does she want?'

'Dorothy's always been busy 'erself. I've never seen 'er just sit an' rest. She expects everyone to be same. I pity 'er daughters.'

Mary thought for a moment. 'I don't think they mind,' she decided. She opened her eyes and sat up. 'Anna even finds time to visit the Gurwoods. I think she's soft on John, but he's only got eyes for Susan. I like Anna,' she said as she yawned. 'She's the best of the bunch. Young Dorothy and Jane must find life hard at Uphall though. They have to help look after baby Richard as well as help out with the cooking.'

'Well,' said Kate smugly, 'I'm glad I'm not up there anymore. I like it 'ere best.' They both smiled. Mary was happy and content but, as often happened at such times, her mind turned to death and misfortune.

'It's terrible what happened to the blacksmith's son,' she whispered, afraid to speak louder in case it tempted fate.

'Aye, Sarah said 'e were scalded by boilin' 'ot broth. 'E were only two years old. Dost tha remember 'ow 'e were born straight after storm? Poor bairn, 'e didn't die straight off. 'E lived for another two days.' They were quiet for a while, imagining the horrors. 'It were a blessin' 'e died,' Kate concluded.

'Couldn't they do anything to save him?'

'Martha shoved 'im in a tub o' cold water at first. Then she'd tried bathin' 'im i' limewater. It were little Elizabeth who ran for Sarah. Phineas was out 'elpin' fix summat up at vicarage. I don't know where other lass was.'

'But couldn't Sarah do anything?'

'She did 'er best no doubt. Martha telled me Sarah 'ad put a thick poultice of oatmeal an' water on 'im an' 'ad been ever so gentle with 'im, seeing as 'e were in such pain. But poor lad 'ad blisters all over 'is body. I tell thee it were a blessin'.'

'But couldn't Sarah help with the pain?'

'Aye. She made sure 'e slept a lot an' gave 'im plenty o' meadowsweet tea to sup.'

Mary's eyes filled with tears.

Kate put down her knitting. 'Well, Mary,' she said, 'no use makin' thassen miserable. Come on. Let's see 'ow curds 'ave drained.'

Mary dried her eyes on her apron. As she stood up to follow Kate, she shook herself to rid her mind of visions of the blacksmith's son.

Kate went straight to the bundle of cloth and opened it up. The curds had lost most of their liquid and had shrunk and become firm. Kate took a piece and bit into it.

'If it squeaks, it's ready,' she said. Satisfied with the curds, she got Mary to help her strain them once more through the cheesecloth. She added salt to taste and pronounced the cheese ready – a soft cheese to be eaten now, not one to be stored.

Mary was puzzled. 'But, Kate, I thought you wanted a cheese press and moulds.'

'I did, but they're for 'arder cheeses. I know a good recipe an' I'll show thee one day.'

That night, as Mary and William lay in bed, Mary thought about her day in the milkhouse. She was excited and couldn't relax, recalling all she'd learnt. She couldn't resist telling William.

'Kate said you can't have women working on cheese if it's their time of the month. It won't set properly. I never knew that. We have to keep the room really clean too.'

William was only half listening. She'd hardly spoken of anything else since he'd come home. He was thinking of his own day.

'That cistern's taken up a lot of time,' he murmured. 'Never knew it would be so hard.'

'And Kate tests to see if a curd is ready by biting it. If it squeaks, it's done.'

'Father thinks we might be able to start harvesting the hay soon. Dickon reckons the dry weather should hold.'

'I think next time we'll make a harder cheese – maybe try and get a good rind on it. Then it'll keep longer.' As if suddenly remembering who was beside her, she added, 'You could have it for your lunches, up in the fields.'

He sighed and turned over. 'Go to sleep, Mary. I'm tired.'

She lay on her back with her hands resting on her stomach, too full of ideas to sleep. She had plans now for pies using cheese pastry. Kate might know of some good recipes, and they could bake together. She sighed happily and snuggled nearer to William. She kissed his shoulder but he was already snoring.

Chapter 20

Mary was soon shown how to make a harder cheese by working butter into the curds. More work was involved as they had to keep breaking up the curds and pouring off the whey, but Mary was eager to use the cheese press at last. It became quite a preoccupation as every so often they had to take the cheese from the press, remove the wet cloth and replace it with a clean, dry one. Eventually the cheese was taken from the press a final time and washed in whey before being laid on a new cloth to dry. Kate then put it on the rack and told Mary she needed to keep turning it.

It wasn't long before a row of cheeses was drying out. They were going to be extra hard as the curds had been cut into tiny pieces. Some had a dry, yellowish rind thanks to Kate's patient replacing of the cloths and turning of the cheeses so they dried evenly. It had been a very worthwhile summer. They had enough cheese to last them till Christmas at least. Mary wondered if they might sell some at Hunmanby market but William's mother was horrified. No daughter-in-law of hers was going to stand in a market and shout out her wares. William was equally adamant. It was even more out of the question now he was a churchwarden and, besides, Mary was heavy with child.

'Look, Mary,' he argued, 'you'll have enough to do once the baby's here. Save your strength. You can't walk to Hunmanby in your condition and you'll be too busy feeding the baby later.' Seeing her face drop, he added, 'We need those cheeses for your lovely pies and pasties. I want them all to myself. You make them – I'll eat them.' He pulled her to him and gave her a kiss.

Once he'd left the house, she and Kate had other ideas. Mary may have been confined to the village, to her house and garden, but she was undaunted. Although *she* couldn't go to the market, there was nothing to prevent Kate. All winter and spring Kate had been knitting stockings and had quite a pile of them ready to sell. Now there were the cheeses too.

Early one Tuesday morning, when it was just growing light, Kate left her room under the roof and sneaked down the ladder. Mary knew of her plan but even she didn't hear Kate leave the house with a basket of cheeses on her arm and a bag of stockings slung over her shoulder.

William never noticed her absence at breakfast as Kate was often out in the field milking the cows. He sat at the table, hunched over his bowl of porridge as usual. Then he grabbed his hat, kissed Mary on the cheek and marched out. Before closing the door he turned round with an afterthought.

'We might be doing more ploughing in the fallow today. If we finish late I'll have supper at Uphall.'

'Don't worry. I've plenty to do. I'll see you later.' Good, she thought – plenty of time to do Kate's jobs as well as her own.

Meanwhile, Kate was trudging through the wet grass on her way to Hunmanby. She wasn't cold but her skirt was sodden round the hem and her hair had turned frizzy in the morning mist. She was having second thoughts, wishing she'd only stockings to sell as the basket of cheeses lay heavy on her arm. It was also the first time she'd ever tried to sell anything and was afraid the regulars would object to her on their patch.

When she arrived at the market, she noticed that the arms on some of the women were as thick as a man's and one woman even had a moustache. Dorothy Jordan had been right about the sort of people who sold their wares – you wouldn't want to argue with them. Their language was foul and many had rough, husky voices, probably, Kate guessed, from smoking too many pipes.

Kate had to decide where best to set down her basket. It was a disadvantage to try and sell both food and woollen goods as the stalls for such items were at different ends of the market place. She opted to go near the cheese stalls but needed to keep well clear of the ugly-looking bunch selling goose eggs nearby. She spread her grey cloak over the ground and set out the cheeses. Then she opened her bag of stockings and let them spill out. She couldn't bring herself to shout out her prices and after half an hour she still hadn't sold anything. Finally, she plucked up the courage to yell out.

'Best 'ard cheese! From Jordan milk'ouse – best 'ard cheeses! Don't miss this fine cheese!' She kept up a similar chant which brought a few people nearer. They only bought some stockings. After another hour, most people were packing up and going home having sold their produce. Kate thought it wasn't much of a market. Times were hard and money was scarce. Most country folk she knew were self-sufficient anyway. Perhaps she'd have done better at Bridlington, but she didn't fancy the long walk.

As she was packing up, she caught a whiff of fish. The smell grew stronger. Looking up, she saw the tawny face of Stinky Skate. He'd sold all his fish and was about to walk back home to Filey. He poked her bag of stockings with the toe of his boot.

'What's i' there? Them's rum cheeses – come i' pairs, do they?'

Kate shrugged. She wasn't in the mood for teasing. The market place was emptying and she just wanted to go home.

'Not sold many, eh?' When he grinned she saw half his teeth were missing. 'If that cheese is any good,' he added, 'maybe I'll exchange it for some skate. Where does tha live? I think I've seen thee somewhere.'

'Reighton,' she answered. ''Ere try a bit o' me cheese.' She took out her knife and cut a thin slice. He smelled it and rubbed it between his grubby fingers before putting it in his mouth. He sucked and chewed for a while.

'Ay, it i'n't bad,' he decided. 'Tomorrow I'll be i' Reighton. Tha can give me a couple o' cheeses. We'll do a deal wi' skate or some other fish, eh?'

Next day, Kate and Mary managed to exchange some surplus cheeses for skate. William did not question why they'd come to have so much fish; he was just glad of the change in diet. Kate went to Martha Wrench and swapped some skate for a keg of small beer. Word about these swaps went round the village. Dorothy Jordan, who often had a feeling that things were going on behind her back, never did get to the bottom of it.

Chapter 21

In early July, Mary went into labour. This time she knew what the pains meant and was in no hurry to send for Sarah Ezard. She'd try and stay calm and wait a few hours. It was so warm and sunny that she went into the garden and walked round and round the apple tree and then up and down the vegetable patch. The weather, instead of lifting her spirits, only served to remind her that a summer birth meant missing the harvest again. As her pains became more frequent, she went back indoors and closed the parlour curtains. She told Kate to boil some water and get fresh linen ready.

'And,' she added, 'I'm going to drink a bottle of Ben's mead. You can join me if you like. I aim to get through this better than last time.'

'I don't think tha should,' Kate warned. 'Sarah Ezard'll want thee wide awake.'

'She's not giving birth. Pass me the bottle and a couple of mugs.' Mary gulped down the mead, determined to finish the bottle before she had to send for Sarah. As she tipped back the last few drops and wiped her mouth she decided it was time.

'Go on then,' she told Kate, 'fetch Sarah. But don't bring any others. I don't want a lot of fuss.' While she waited for Kate to return, she had second thoughts about the mead. It lay heavy on her stomach and she was afraid she'd be sick.

Sarah smelled the drink on Mary's breath immediately and sighed; women nowadays couldn't stand pain like they used to. As Mary's waters broke and the contractions came quickly, she told her to kneel on the bed.

Mary prayed she wouldn't puke. The mead did not assuage the worst pains but did help her relax between them. Soon she had the urge to strain hard. To her relief, the baby slipped out quite easily, and she waited to hear it cry.

'It's a daughter tha's got,' Sarah announced, slapping the baby and making her bawl. 'She's got a good pair o' lungs.'

Mary still felt sick and was glad to get off her knees and lay on the bed to rest. As she watched the baby being cleaned, she hoped the girl would be stronger than the boy she'd lost.

'Kate,' she said. 'Run and tell William and then fetch my mother and Elizabeth.'

When the women returned, Mary had already been washed and was lying with the baby asleep beside her. They tiptoed into the dark room and peered at the swaddled child. Only the head was visible, very pink and with a lot of black hair. Elizabeth's eyes welled up. Her mother put an arm round her.

'Don't worry. It'll be *thy* turn soon. These things often take time.'

Elizabeth didn't reply. She wiped her eyes and forced a smile.

Her mother made a suggestion. 'Elizabeth, why don't you stay with Mary while I 'elp Sarah an' Kate i' kitchen?'

Once alone with Mary, Elizabeth confided her fears. 'I don't know when I'll ever have a child or *if* I'll ever have one. You get with child so easily, so quickly.'

Mary didn't take her seriously. 'Don't be silly. Of course you'll have one. Like mother says, sometimes it just takes time.' Elizabeth shrugged, unconvinced, but Mary had an idea. 'Try on my shoes. Go on – they're under the bed. Put them on and have a walk round in them. It's a trick I've heard to help you conceive.'

Elizabeth did this with little interest and less hope. She looked down at her feet, wondering how to explain without being disloyal to her husband.

'It's Robert,' she said at last.

'What about Robert?' Mary asked. 'Well …?' she asked again. 'What about Robert?'

'He … well, he sits up late and reads a lot. The Bible mostly, but George Gurwood lent him another book on Protestant martyrs.'

'Well – so what? How does that affect *you*?'

'He *reads* all the time. He doesn't do anything else ... you know ...'

'What, never?' asked Mary in amazement.

'Well, I wouldn't go that far ...' She looked down at her feet again. 'Sometimes he does, but ...' Tears came into her eyes. 'I'll never have a child at this rate.'

Mary didn't know what to say. Robert was renowned for his puritanical ways. Perhaps the Gurwoods could help since their marriage was such a success.

'How about if I speak to the vicar's wife?' Mary offered.

'Oh, no! For God's sake, don't!'

'But I'm sure she'd understand and want to help. She could have a word with her husband and then he'd speak to Robert.'

'No!' Elizabeth shouted. Mary looked at Elizabeth's feet and shook her head. It was hopeless. Elizabeth took off the shoes and placed them back under the bed. 'Don't say anything to William, please,' she begged.

'All right. I'm sorry. Come and give me a hug. I promise I won't tell a soul.'

William was glad to hear the birth had gone well and was happy for the girl to be named Ann after Mary's mother. Now that he was banned from the house, he could stay at Uphall for the next few weeks and get the cistern finished. The clay work was completed and the cistern roofed over. Gutters were fixed to the barn and a fall pipe to allow rain water to enter the cistern near the bottom; that way, William's father explained, the surface water wouldn't be disturbed. William was impressed. They could now raise water using a bucket on a rope and roller, just like a well, with the extra advantage of having it close by in the yard. The maids would no longer have to traipse back and forth to the hill behind the church to get water from Knox Well – providing, of course, there was plenty of rain to fill the cistern.

To Mary's relief the baby took her feed properly and appeared quite well, but Mary became obsessed with draughts coming into the house. Though it was high summer, she insisted that all windows be kept shut and the baby protected at all times from the outside air. She'd convinced herself that Thomas's death had been due to bad air from the stagnant pond down the lane or to the flies that hung round the milk bucket.

Her house became a fortress. She sent a message to William to buy yards of thick woollen cloth for curtains to hang behind the front and back doors. She'd asked him for dark red, but he returned with cheap blue material – the sort normally reserved for servants' clothes. She had to concede it was thick enough for its purpose.

The rest of the village was scornful. One day, Ann Huskisson was standing by the forge with Martha Wrench. Kate happened to be passing by and heard them talking. Martha stood with her arms folded.

'What on earth is Mary Jordan doin' wi' curtains behind doors i' middle o' summer?'

'I don't know. She gets above 'ersen like some other Jordans I know.'

Kate stopped and defended Mary. 'She's lost one bairn. Tha can't expect 'er not be extra fussy over next one. She'll be all right soon, tha'll see.'

She marched away before they could answer. But Mary's obsession was a worry. All Mary did was sit in bed or in her chair, holding the baby and watching it. At night Mary would wake up suddenly and rush to the crib to see if Ann was still breathing. Then she'd feel the baby's face and neck to see if they were warm. Kate thought the poor baby was too hot if anything. Even though it was summer, Ann was swaddled up tightly. The room was stifling, but Mary would not allow any fresh air in. She did relax a little after the baptism and Kate persuaded her to take the curtains from the doors. Last year Mary had fretted about not being allowed outside during her confinement. This year she was quite content to feed and clean and watch her baby, all the time indoors.

Kate remained concerned and wondered if Mary would still want to work in the milkhouse. All Mary wanted to talk about now was how well little Ann was drinking her milk, and how the baby's eyes followed her. One afternoon Kate watched as Mary sank into her nursing chair and loosened her bodice to feed the baby. Now Mary would only have time for the baby yet again. Feeling left out, Kate found the room suddenly too hot and stuffy. She made an excuse to go out.

Left alone, Mary braced herself for the pain as Ann got excited and rooted around. The baby girl grabbed a nipple and held it between her gums as tight as a vice. Mary winced. There was the familiar excruciating tingle as if the milk was being forced out through a thousand needles. She never quite got used to it and gripped the chair and banged her feet up and down until the milk began to flow and the baby settled into a rhythmical suck. Now she could relax. Such moments were a pleasure. Her existence was justified and she certainly couldn't be doing any other jobs. To be able to sit and think without interruption was a rare treat, and to know you were being a good mother at the same time was heaven. At this moment everyone else would be busy in the fields. This year she didn't mind. Here she was, safe indoors, quiet and peaceful with her baby for company. She looked at Ann's closed eyes with their long, dark lashes and sighed with contentment. This little girl connected her with all the past generations of mothers and daughters. She imagined delicate but beautiful golden links in a chain, stretching back in time, with Ann as the latest link.

That summer many villagers were sick and had loose bowels, but the very young and the elderly suffered the most. Mary's daughter had been fine for over three weeks before she too became ill. Kate offered to spend more time at the house so she could help more.

'Dorothy Jordan doesn't want any sickness at Up'all,' she said. 'I think she's quite 'appy to be rid of me an' any illness I might bring.'

Mary needed all the help she could get as the baby began to vomit up all her feeds and had dreadful diarrhoea. Ten times a day Mary or Kate had to clean up the mess. The house was beginning to stink. After a few days Mary became really worried.

One afternoon, when Kate was out milking, she thought her baby would never stop crying. She got a screw of rag, dipped it in sugar-water and put it in Ann's mouth. Having quietened the baby, she held her close and, despite her confinement, rushed out of the house and slammed the door shut. She headed straight up the hill to Sarah Ezard's and barged in without knocking. Sarah was busy decanting some steaming liquid from her cauldron into various sized pots but stopped on seeing the look on Mary's face. She wiped her hands down her apron and pushed some stray grey hairs back under her bonnet.

'What's up, Mary?'

'I can't stop the flux. It's not me, it's the baby.'

'Let's 'ave a look at 'er.' Mary unwrapped Ann and passed her to Sarah. The baby hung limp in her arms and looked very pale with sunken eyes. 'What's 'er water like?'

'She hasn't passed much today. What there was looked more like apple juice – dark yellow.'

Just then the baby woke up. Sarah tried to gain her attention but she didn't respond at all – she just opened her mouth and cried weakly. There were no tears. Sarah noted the dry lips and, on parting them, saw that the mouth inside was sticky. There was no proper spit. Sarah was afraid that any help given would be too late. She passed the baby back and looked Mary in the eye.

'Tha bairn needs water, an' fast. I'll mix up some water wi' sugar an' a pinch o' salt.' While Sarah warmed it up she added, 'Just feed 'er a spoon at a time but do it often an' keep tryin' wi' tha milk.'

'Is there nothing else we can try?'

'Aye, it might not 'elp but I'll crush some garlic an' bind it on 'er belly.'

While the sugar and salt were dissolving, Sarah pounded the garlic. The baby squirmed listlessly when the juicy pulp was fixed round her thin body. Mary thought she was clutching at straws but thanked Sarah anyway and took the bottle of water. She wrapped the baby up once more and walked back home in a daze, her throat choked with tears.

That night the baby died in her sleep. Deep down, Mary knew her daughter was dead before she even touched her, yet still could hardly believe it had happened again. She collapsed onto her knees sobbing. Kate heard the noise and came down the ladder to find Mary in the candlelight holding the baby to her breast. She knelt down beside her and they rocked to and fro together. There was nothing to be said. They stayed like that until dawn and then Kate made them each a warm drink. Later she went to Uphall to tell William.

Mary's mother and sister arrived and stayed all morning and, when the time came, helped Mary get through the funeral. People called by with commiserations. George and Susanna Gurwood stayed a while to offer words of comfort, but Mary couldn't recall afterwards what they'd said. Old Ben visited and left a jar of honey.

For Mary, the days passed as if she was in another world. Her confinement was over but there was nothing to show for it. William returned home but couldn't console her. He said he regretted the time spent on the water cistern yet, after seeing the baby only once, at the baptism, how could he mourn for a child he'd never known? When he spent any time alone with Mary, she always ended up crying. Her milk was still coming through – a cruel reminder of the futility of her life. William cuddled her and kissed her and sometimes she responded and held onto him, vulnerable and weepy. At other times she pushed him away coldly. At dawn, when he set off for the harvest, she clung on to him and wanted him to stay at home.

William breathed a sigh of relief whenever he left the house and got into the open air. Mary's erratic behaviour was confusing. It was much better to be outside and fully occupied with the men, his brothers and Dickon. He knew where he was with them and received plenty of sympathy from husbands who'd been through such times themselves.

It was Kate who once again rescued Mary. As soon as all the harvesting was done she suggested they make the blue woollen curtains into gowns. Mary thought this a sensible idea, but she herself would not wear them. Kate could have the blue gowns – she deserved them. That autumn they worked together, quietly pinning and stitching by the fire. William was pleased to see them so occupied. He leant back in his chair smoking his pipe, watching their heads move in unison. He let their quiet conversation wash over him until it was far too dark to sew anymore and time for bed.

It was late in October when Mary realised she was with child yet again.

Part Two

Love and Lust

Chapter 22

The harvest that year was good and, once it was over, the whole village began to relax. Each day at supper time, William reported to Mary how the lads at Uphall were getting more restless as the November hirings approached.

'They're getting rough. There's one trick they play – to pick on someone, rush at them and force them over the fold yard wall. It's the ones who've decided to leave who are the worst. And it's Tom who's suffering. They know he wants to stay in Reighton.'

'Poor Tom,' she said. 'He's not as strong as some of them.'

'Well, it's not just a question of brute strength. Timing's everything. If you catch someone off guard, you can easily up-end them.'

'At least Dickon'll look out for him.'

'Dickon can't be there all the time.'

One morning, as Tom was walking to the stable, one of the older and stronger lads charged at him head down without any warning and shouldered him up onto the wall in one move. Tom's breath was knocked out of him and, before he knew it, he was lying flat on his back in the dung heap on the other side. He gasped for air and lay still as clouds above him floated slowly by. Faces peered over the wall to laugh at him and gloat. William's brother, Francis, was one of them and didn't lend a hand; he just smirked. The lad who'd pushed Tom over shouted down at him.

'I've seen lasses wicker 'an thoo. Thoo's nowt but a windlestraw.'

'Aye,' sniggered another, 'an' lick-spittlin' up to Jordans won't 'elp. Thoo'd best move on.'

But Tom wanted to stay. He liked living at Uphall, sleeping among the stores in the loft, and he liked the Jordan family, especially Anna and the children. It suited him in Reighton and he was building up a good working relationship with Dickon.

Unbeknown to them, Anna had been watching from the kitchen window. She sighed and shook her head and, when the lads had gone about their work, went to help Tom clean himself up. He blushed and mumbled a thank you. She did not embarrass him further by asking questions and soon left him alone. Her kindness made him more determined than ever to stay and prove himself worthy of Uphall.

Now the sheaves were stored away, William had more time on his hands to chat and enjoy a pipe. Late one afternoon he stood in the top field leaning over the gate with Matthew. It was still warm enough to be without a coat, and they leant against the gate smoking and watching idly while oxen and horses picked over the stubble. For a while they said nothing, at ease in each other's company. They gazed over Filey Bay at the sea with its stripes of turquoise and jade. William thought that Matthew looked as calm as the sea and had probably recovered from the loss of his wife. He decided to confide in him over the loss of his son and then a daughter.

'Do you think it's me that's at fault?' he asked. 'Do you think there's some weakness in me, that I'm not man enough somehow?'

Matthew laughed. 'I didn't call you shorty for nothing. But no,' he added more seriously, 'I don't think for a moment it's that. You don't have any problem getting Mary with child. Now, Elizabeth and Robert – that's another matter, or I should say, another story.'

William grimaced at the pun. They puffed on their pipes and turned to watch the clouds grow pink in the west, still speculating about Robert Storey's lack of success. William looked so solemn that Matthew gave him a hefty push. William's mood changed instantly. He smiled and recalled the times they'd wrestled as boys. He stuck out his leg to trip Matthew.

'Want a fight, do you?' Matthew challenged.

'Why not?' They knocked out their pipes and began to wrestle. It was like old times with neither getting the upper hand. After a while they gave up and lay panting on their backs. They saw the sky was darkening and began to laugh. It was good to be playing the fool.

The longer nights gave Matthew's sister, Elizabeth, more opportunity to become pregnant. Each day as she worked in the kitchen, she imagined different ways of seducing her reluctant husband. As she rolled out the suet pastry she recalled their first night together. When he'd tried to enter her, he'd pushed in the wrong place and she'd had to guide him in. It had then all been over in a minute. Afterwards, she was hot and sore inside. On subsequent occasions he'd still needed guiding in and it had always been over far too quickly. She was eager for kisses afterwards and wanted to roll around with him and demonstrate how much she loved him. She daydreamed of what she'd do if he'd relax for once and let her do the loving. The trouble was that, once he'd finished, he'd almost leap out of her, cough as if embarrassed, then turn over and fall asleep.

Robert never did fall asleep immediately. Instead, he would lie almost rigid next to her, trying not to let their bodies touch, his eyes staring into the blackness. He could not explain how disgusted he was and how lost and empty he felt whenever he and Elizabeth tried for a child. The smell of women repulsed him and looking after his old father and having to deal with the old man's private functions did nothing to enhance any desire for Elizabeth. He continued to tackle his fears of death and decay by prayer, by reading and by fasting. Not only did he eat less, he tried to curb all desires of the flesh and focus on his spiritual life.

Elizabeth reacted differently. When she helped Robert's father drink his soup, or held him over the bed pan, she realised how tenuous life was. The more time she spent with frailty and illness, the more she wanted to assert her own healthy desires and live life to the full. But she knew it would be a defeat for Robert if he succumbed to her charms.

Robert's sister, the vicar's wife, often visited them. Susanna Gurwood knew what he was like and was sorry for Elizabeth. She remembered only too well how Robert, even as a child, had always shunned the rough fun and games enjoyed by others. He'd always been different and aloof, preferring to read quietly or go for long walks alone. Susanna would have liked to help Elizabeth look after her father, but she was far too busy with her own family. She wanted to befriend Elizabeth yet, no matter how much she hinted at Robert's character, Elizabeth would not confide in her. As a last resort, and behind Elizabeth's back, Susanna asked Sarah Ezard to pay a visit.

Instead of calling round, Sarah stopped Elizabeth in the street one morning and reminded her of an old superstition.

'If thoo wants a bairn, tha needs to get 'im to piss through 'is weddin' ring. That should work. Try it.'

'Thank you,' said Elizabeth, puzzled by the sudden advice. She'd never dare ask Robert to do such a thing. They were never that intimate. She'd never even seen him without clothes, and only touched his body in the dark. She could only continue as she did, care for both Robert and his father and hope for better times.

Susanna Gurwood also hoped for better times. She now spent much of each day nursing her mother-in-law, Maria. George reminded her that, in her youth, his mother had been a kind, thoughtful person. However, now she was bed-bound and crippled with arthritis she was quite spiteful. She accused Susanna of stealing her necklace and made it clear that she never wanted to see her granddaughters again. Susanna had to carry out her duties regardless. When she helped Maria sit up in bed for her meal, the old woman glared with cold hatred. Her mother-in-law was stubborn and almost had to be force-fed. Susanna found it increasingly difficult to deal with the malignant look she received whenever the bed linen was changed or when Maria was washed. The old woman's language grew coarser by the day and, for the mother of a vicar, she knew an amazing number of blasphemies and curses.

Susanna was relieved that at least she could keep Maria separate in her own chamber; that way her daughters had no contact, but it led to over-crowding. There was only one other upstairs chamber and the downstairs parlour left for Susanna, her husband and their eight children to sleep in. Also, another baby was due in the spring. She hoped it would be her last.

Chapter 23

1706-7

At Uphall the rowdier lads left in November, but the new batch that arrived included a bully – Simeon. As if drawn by a magnet, William's brother Francis took to him straightaway. As for Simeon, he thought he'd landed on his feet to be so well in with a Jordan. Dickon, with all his experience, was wary and tried to warn Tom.

'Watch out for yon Simeon. I don't like looks of 'im. Mind thassen, Tom. That lad 'as trouble written right across 'is fore'ead.'

It wasn't just Tom who needed to watch out. Simeon had a cruel streak and, like Francis, was only too ready to pass the blame onto others when accused of negligence or poor workmanship. Francis and Simeon liked to pair off in the morning when work was allotted, and somehow managed to get the lighter jobs. William and his brother John ended up with the muck-spreading on the furthest fields and, when they got back to Uphall, Francis and Simeon would already be lounging about smoking their pipes.

After a month of this, Dickon grew resentful on Tom's behalf. He could see that Tom was working as hard as ever, up before dawn every morning to kibble the grain for the cattle and muck out the sheds. The lad was thoughtful and saved any cow dung that had dried on the boards for use later as fuel. He also fed the horses before he had his own breakfast and groomed them gently while they were distracted munching their chaff and oats. He was worth ten of Simeon and Francis. Being in charge of the horses and oxen, Dickon made sure that neither Francis nor Simeon was trusted with these precious animals.

Late one morning in December, when work was slack, Dickon heard a commotion behind the barn. When he went to see what all the fuss was about, he found Francis and Simeon pelting a chicken with sticks and stones. They'd tethered the hen to a stake and had taken bets as to who could kill it first. Dickon didn't hesitate. He strode through their barrage of stones and untied the hen. His face was dark with anger as he growled at Francis.

'If tha larks was bulls, tha'd soon feel 'is 'orns.' As he passed Simeon he spat on the ground. Thinking they'd watch out in future, he did not report them.

Not long after this, Tom saw them tormenting the boar. Francis and Simeon had a catapult each and were aiming at its testicles. Tom tried to hide from them and intended to go and tell Dickon, but they spotted him.

'Get him,' shouted Francis. 'Get him before he tells on us … the little squealer.'

Simeon was onto Tom before he got far and dragged him back by his hair. There was nothing Tom could do. His scalp was stinging and the more he struggled, the more his head hurt. Simeon threw him onto the frozen ground and kicked him in the groin. Tom doubled up in agony, his eyes bulging, and retched. He didn't care what they did anymore so long as they left him alone. Francis bent over and threatened him.

'Tell a soul and you're finished here at Uphall.' He kicked Tom's boots. 'Did you hear me?' Tom managed to nod. He was still winded and could hardly move.

'I think 'e wants 'is mammy,' sneered Simeon. 'Look – I can see tears in 'is little eyes.' It was then that Francis's sister, Anna, walked across the yard to draw water from the cistern.

'We'd best be off,' whispered Francis. 'I don't trust her. She might tell Dickon.' Simeon was reluctant to go. 'Come on!' urged Francis. 'Leave Tom. We'll fix him another day.' They sauntered off, whistling a tune.

Anna didn't have any idea what had happened and Tom wouldn't tell her. She knelt beside him, ignoring the dirt and the cold, and put her hand on his head. He leapt aside as if shot; the hairs on his head were like hot wires. Not knowing where he was hurt, she helped him to his feet.

'I'm all right,' he mumbled. 'Let me alone. I can see to meself.'

'Let me take you in to mother. You look as if you've had a nasty fall.'

'Nay, I'll go to Dickon. Leave me be.'

Though it was shameful to be found on the ground like that, he'd have loved to have stayed there longer, preferably with his head in her lap. He'd liked a good many girls in the village, but Anna Jordan, now eighteen years old, was turning out to be a splendid young woman. He brushed the frost and dirt off his coat and breeches, thanked her, and limped off towards the stable.

He found Dickon sitting astride the bench oiling the harnesses. As Tom walked in, the warm smells of horse sweat and linseed oil were a comfort. He breathed in deeply, relaxed a little and ran his fingers down the leather straps hanging by the door. Dickon looked up and noticed the tears in Tom's eyes.

'What's up, lad?'

'Nowt.'

'Get some more linseed then, an' get crackin'.' Tom sat down next to Dickon and began oiling the straps with a rag. 'Mind tha soaks it in well. Don't leave gaps neither.'

They rubbed in the oil with a certain rhythm and, every so often, bent each strap back and forth to let the oil seep into the middle of the leather. It was quiet except for the horses' hooves shuffling in the straw.

Tom eventually broke the silence. 'I'm afraid I've made enemies of Francis an' Simeon.'

'Wouldn't take much.'

'Dickon, they're out to get me.'

Dickon laid down his strap and put a hand on Tom's shoulder. 'I'll see tha's all right.'

Tom was not convinced.

The winter months proved Tom correct. There were many times when Francis or Simeon, or worse still, the pair of them, found Tom alone. They knew his working routine and found innumerable ways to make life difficult. They'd hide the tools he needed or break the handles so that even Dickon began to think Tom careless. They'd sometimes lie in wait and stick a leg out to trip him or, when it was dark, lay a log across his path. It was going to be a long time until next November and, even then, Simeon might stay on.

The bullying did not go unnoticed. Anna Jordan was very active around the yards. Her younger sisters spent their days looking after their young brothers and did most of the cooking and mending with their mother; this meant that Anna was free to help in the milkhouse, brew ale in the buttery and look after the poultry. It was Anna who often noticed what was going on around Uphall – who was doing what, and when. Many times she'd seen Francis and Simeon sneak off together and guessed they'd be up to no good. She decided to speak to Tom and find out the extent of any bullying.

One morning in January, Anna got up earlier than usual. She knew that Francis and Simeon would be scarce since ploughing had begun again. They'd be looking for easier work, but Tom would be seeing to the oxen. She left the house and crossed the yard. Icicles hung from the roofs and dripped steadily into pools. Following a glimmer of light, she found Tom in the barn raising water from the cistern. He touched his hat in greeting and called out through the gloom.

'Thoo's up early. I'm just findin' some warmer water for oxen.'

'I'll come with you, Tom. I've been wanting to talk to you.'

His heart slammed into his stomach. He carried the bucket to the shed and his hands shook as he poured water into the trough. When he began putting feed into the manger, Anna moved into the light shed by the lantern.

'Don't think I'm interfering,' she said, her breath steaming in the frosty air, 'but I know what's been going on between you and Francis.' Tom kept his head down, pretending to check the animals' legs. 'Something has to be done.'

Still staring at the legs, Tom muttered, 'Don't see what. I'm just an 'ired lad. This is Francis's place. 'E can do what 'e likes.'

'No, Tom, he can't. I won't tell my father but, if you don't mind, I'm going to see William. He'll find a way to stop Francis – and that bastard Simeon.'

Surprised by Anna's language, Tom looked up and raised his eyebrows. Her hood had slipped and lay round her neck showing off her chestnut hair and rosy cheeks. Her brown eyes glittered in the light from the lantern. He wanted to throw his arms round her and hold her tight but knew it was impossible. She suddenly leant towards him and gave him a quick kiss on the cheek. Then she was off, back across the yard to the house. Alone again in the dimly lit shed, a huge smile spread over his face and, despite the cold, he felt a growing warmth inside.

Chapter 24

1707

Anna Jordan went to see William late one afternoon just before it got dark. Mary and Kate were surprised to see her as she didn't visit often. They got her to take her pattens and cloak off and go in the kitchen to get warm. Kate brought out oatcakes and heated up some ale. Anna looked uncomfortable and coughed as the northeast wind blew smoke from the fire.

'William's not back yet,' said Mary. 'It was him you wanted?'

'Yes. Sorry I don't get to see you often. There's always so much going on at Uphall. I hear you're with child again.'

Mary patted her stomach and nodded but changed the subject quickly. 'Have you seen much of John Gurwood recently?'

'No.' Anna blushed. They were quiet for a moment as Kate poured out the drinks. They bunched up together on the bench at the side of the fire away from the smoke, their hands curled round their pots of hot ale. Anna kicked off her shoes and held her stockinged feet to the fire. She wriggled her toes.

'Mind tha doesn't get chilblains,' warned Kate.

'I'll risk it. It's freezing out there today.'

Just then they heard William at the door. Mary went to help him pull off his boots and told him that Anna was waiting to see him. This came as a surprise since Anna could see him any day at Uphall. He paddled into the kitchen.

'What's up, Anna? Has something happened?'

'No,' she began, 'I've come about Tom.' He sat on the opposite bench, none the wiser. 'Don't you know that

Francis, and that Simeon, have been making life hell for him since November?'

'No – I haven't noticed. I'm usually working with John, and Dickon's never mentioned anything.'

'He wouldn't, would he? He's always telling us he saves his wind to cool his porridge.'

William knew what his brother was like, and trusted Anna, yet bullying seemed rather extreme even for Francis. Anna was hurt when she saw the look of doubt on his face.

'Don't you believe me?' she asked. 'I can tell you plenty.' She got off the bench and stood in front of him, her hands on her hips. 'Remember that time the shovel handle was split? Francis and Simeon broke it and blamed Tom. Remember when Dickon's horse linctus went missing, then was found spilled round where Tom worked? They'd rubbed his face in it.' William was surprised. She carried on. 'Remember when Tom wouldn't wear his hat, even in December? It's because they'd pulled him by his hair and it hurt to have anything touch it.' She flopped back down on the bench, out of breath. 'I could say more. They're brutes, Francis and Simeon. And they need stopping.' She stared at them in turn as she calmed down a little.

Mary and Kate looked on, wide-eyed. They'd never seen Anna in such a state. It must be bad, they thought, for Anna to see William in secret, and her red face spoke the truth. William was silent for a while and then came to a decision.

'This needs careful planning. I want father to see for himself what's going on. I want to catch them out. Leave it to me, Anna, and don't tell Tom. He mustn't suspect anything.'

William bided his time, waiting for the right opportunity. Now that he was aware of the situation, he kept his eyes and ears open. He also confided in his brother, John. Their chance came in mid-February. The lower meadows were under water and the ditches needed scouring. This was the kind of job that Francis and Simeon would avoid. William knew that the rest of the lads who were not working on the ditches and hedges would be out ploughing with Dickon. Tom happened to be staying behind at Uphall with William's father to tend a sick cow.

William and John set off with their trenching spades as if to go down the hill to the meadows but, when they got there, they left instructions with the lads and then went back home via Oxtrope Lane and the main street.

Francis and Simeon were supposed to be repairing hedges behind the farm, but they had their eyes on the cow shed, waiting for Francis's father to leave. After about half an hour Tom was left alone in the shed. He was unaware of John, now outside and hiding below the tiny window. William was lurking nearby, also out of view, by the barn. Francis and Simeon strolled casually back into the yard, looking about to check they were alone. They walked into the cow shed.

Tom's heart sank. Another day, another tormenting.

'Now then,' jeered Simeon, 'what's tha goin' to do if yon cow gets worse?'

'She won't get worse,' Tom muttered, but the cow had a serious mouth infection brought on by feeding on rough hay. He was worried because the best of the hay had been eaten long ago and even the poor stuff would run out before the new grass came through. The cow drooled saliva over Tom's boots and eyed the group of men mournfully. The infection had taken a strong hold and the cow's tongue was swollen and painful. Francis grabbed its head and prised open its jaws. He pulled back as the foul breath hit his face. Simeon laughed and stepped forward to poke the tongue. It was hard and had ulcers.

'It's got Wooden Tongue,' Francis diagnosed smugly. 'What's my father going to do? Slaughter it?'

'Not yet,' answered Tom. 'We might try blood-lettin'.'

'What's that? Speak up, lad,' shouted Simeon as he nipped the cow's tongue between his fingers. The cow bellowed loudly in pain and stepped back onto Tom's foot. Tom let out a yell. Even his winter boots were no defence against a hoof with the weight of a cow behind it.

Waiting outside, William heard the noise and, suspecting Francis had begun something, went to find his father. He brought him into the yard on the pretext that the cow was worse and Tom needed help. As they approached the shed, they could hear voices but did not know what was happening.

Simeon had Tom on his knees under the cow's belly. The damp straw reeked of urine and the cow, unnerved by all the attention, suddenly loosened its bowels. Tom did not have time to move away. The smell was bad enough, but the dark green liquid splashed into his face. He heard them laughing. Simeon held him down with his boot, then pulled Tom's arms behind his back and pressed him closer to the udders.

'Come on, Tommy boy, drink up.'

'Suck them, then, like a wee bairn,' urged Francis and made slurping noises. Tom was just thinking he was not going to get out of this when John shouted through the window at the same time as William and his father entered the shed. Francis and Simeon went pale. Simeon let go of Tom and backed away. Francis hardly dare look his father in the eye.

'Son, get out of 'ere an' get into kitchen. I'll be there soon enough. Simeon, get back to work.'

Tom, still on his knees in the fouled straw, watched bewildered as Simeon barged past William and had the cheek to look him full in the face as he went out. Francis followed him, his eyes to the ground. As soon as his tormentors had left, Tom straightened himself up and tried to brush off the straw stuck to his wet knees. He started to leave but William stopped him.

'Wait. Father needs to know what happened.'

'I saw it all,' John intervened, and explained in detail what he'd seen and heard. William added other tales that he'd heard from Anna.

Tom was amazed that Anna had known so much and had cared enough to tell someone. He wiped a tear from his soiled face and limped out of the door. As he passed

William's father, he thought his master looked tired and much older than his years.

Francis Jordan was ashamed of his son yet didn't say another word. He turned slowly and trudged out of the shed. Instead of going straight into the house, he went across the muddy yard to look out over the fields. He was wondering how he could have bred such different sons. His wife would need to know about Francis as he was now thinking of a way to remove him from Reighton, preferably in a way that would save face for all concerned. His mind made up, he walked back to the house.

His wife stood in the kitchen over a huge pot of soup, stirring it slowly, unaware of the upset. Francis was sitting by the fire, already smoking a pipe as if nothing had happened.

'I've been thinkin',' his father said as he sat down opposite, 'per'aps tha needs to work away – get some work at another place.'

Dorothy turned round and looked from one to the other; it didn't make sense.

Her son's pipe dropped from his mouth. 'What place?' he asked.

'I was thinkin' maybe at Argam wi' thy uncle. 'E needs a strong, young man. Maybe, if tha does well, tha can carry on there when 'e's past workin'.'

Francis had little choice. His father's word was law. It was a form of exile, but he didn't want to work anymore with his brothers and Tom and Dickon.

'Can I take Simeon with me?' he dared to ask.

'Nay. Thoo's bad for each other. I'll send 'im somewhere else – maybe to a farm i' Bartindale. We'll manage very well without 'im.'

Dorothy looked again from one to the other and couldn't believe what she'd heard. She stirred the soup and kept her peace for once. Just then Anna walked into the kitchen. Her father explained about her brother's move to Argam. Francis noticed she didn't look too surprised and suspected bitterly that she was in on it somehow. He determined to get his own back one day.

Chapter 25

Although Anna Jordan had defended and helped Tom, she did not find him attractive. She only had eyes for John Gurwood, the vicar's son. In church she'd stare at the back of his head thinking that, if she willed it enough, he'd turn to see her and smile. She thought he was kind as well as handsome. She knew that he read the Bible to his old grandmother every afternoon, her favourite parts over and over again.

Many times that winter, Anna Jordan had visited the Gurwoods hoping to see John, unaware that his sisters and mother felt sorry for her. They knew John did not return her affections. Often he'd make himself scarce when she called. She was made welcome at their house partly because she was a lot less flighty than her cousin Susan, who was John's real preference. Also, Anna provided light relief for the vicar's daughters who suffered with their old grandmother living upstairs.

Anna heard from Sarah Ezard that the woman was getting worse.

''Er eyes are all milky wi' cataracts,' she told her one day. 'An' 'er 'ands are knotted up like tree roots.'

Though the grandmother was in pain and everyone tried to be generous, Anna could tell their patience was wearing thin. Susanna kept her daughters away from the woman's foul language and aimed to keep the girls busy downstairs. As a fire could be lit in the parlour, she decided they'd all make a patchwork quilt there together.

One cold afternoon Anna was at the Gurwoods and sat patiently with the girls while Susanna explained about the quilt.

'You know we have to sleep five girls in one bed now, because of grandmother, so we need a quilt large enough to reach over. I've already joined two worn sheets together for the backing and I've been saving bits of cloth.' She held up a finger. 'Never throw anything away. It's all useful one day.' She sighed as she pointed to a chest on the floor. 'That belonged to your grandmother. She never threw anything out. It's full of old bits of curtains and gowns.'

Susanna opened the chest and tipped all the materials onto the floor. The girls gasped. It didn't matter that some pieces were faded and worn thin, there was such a variety. Little Priscilla, only two years old, jumped up and ran through them, clutching handfuls and tossing them into the air to fall on her head.

Jane, the eldest, took charge. She asked each of the girls their favourite colour and then suggested they each make a part of the cover in their chosen shade. Anna waited until they'd all made their choice. The four older girls had picked red, blue, yellow and green. Elizabeth, now six years old, was left till last. Anna asked her if she had a favourite colour.

'Black,' Elizabeth said. The others groaned.

'You can't have black,' said Jane, 'it's too funereal.'

'She's just saying it to be awkward,' said Cecilia.

'I want black,' pouted Elizabeth.

'You don't have to decide straight away,' said Anna, 'maybe you haven't seen all the bits yet.' She knelt on the floor and rummaged through the pile, looking for unusual colours. She managed to get Elizabeth's attention and persuaded her to pick out anything she liked. The others waited. Cecilia yawned. After what seemed ages, Elizabeth had picked out a dozen pieces and most of them were shades of pink and brown.

'Are you happy now?' Jane asked, impatient to start. Elizabeth looked at Anna, wondering if she dared return to black.

'Yes, I think we're both happy with these,' said Anna. Elizabeth took Anna's hand and nodded. She was glad Anna was there – she was kinder than her sisters.

All through the wintry days of February, the girls gathered to make the bed cover. The wind rattled the door and rain and sleet lashed against the windows, but it remained cosy in the parlour. They enjoyed cutting the fabrics into strips, while the three youngest girls played with their dolls. Before long they were busy over-sewing the edges, chattering together as they stitched and relishing any gossip. They sat open-mouthed as Anna told stories about Francis and Simeon. They asked her if Elizabeth Storey was having any luck yet with a baby. They knew they shouldn't but listened eagerly when Anna told them of ways to conceive a child.

'You can put your shoes up the chimney,' she informed them, 'or under the thatch – near any house entrance, in fact.' She enjoyed their attention. 'And Sarah Ezard says you can boil woollen yarn, then mix the water with ashes and sit over it. But Dickon says you're to drink goats' milk and eat goats' b …' She reduced her voice to a whisper so the young ones wouldn't hear. 'Bollocks.' They all giggled.

Jane was thinking about procreation as she sewed her strips together. 'Anna,' she asked, 'do you think it's true that men carry the seed of the baby and women are just the place for it to grow?'

They all looked up from their sewing, believing Anna would know the answer.

'Yes, it's true,' she replied. 'At least that's what I've heard. But look at you all – every one of you, except for Jane, looks exactly like your mother. How can that be? If your father just passed on the seed to your mother, then you'd all look like him.'

This intrigued them for a while and then Cecilia had an idea. 'Maybe, by the time the baby is born, all that growing inside the mother makes the baby look more like her. It could be.' No one knew. They shrugged and moved on to other topics.

As she stitched, Anna kept one eye on the doorway hoping to see John enter and say hello. Sometimes when he'd finished reading to his grandmother, he'd sit with them in the parlour. This was what Anna looked forward to, especially if he could be persuaded to play the fiddle. He knew plenty of tunes and they could all sing together as they sewed their strips. At such times Anna couldn't concentrate on her work and gazed instead at John's face. He had such a fine brow and strong chin, and above his full lips was the beginning of a moustache.

One afternoon, while John was playing his fiddle in the parlour, his mother listened from the kitchen. She sat near the fire, leaning against the warm wall to ease her aching back. Her baby was due in the spring and, with all the extra work involved in looking after her mother-in-law, she was worn out. It was heaven to stop work for a while, close her eyes and listen to the girls singing in the next room.

In early March, the quilt was nearing completion and Susanna Gurwood's baby was due any day. She found it so difficult now to deal with her mother-in-law. She could hardly lift her up and hated to ask her husband or John for help. For days old Maria refused to eat and would only have sips of water. She kept bringing up a foul-smelling black liquid as if going rotten from the inside. Susanna couldn't help but retch at times. The first visits in the morning were the worst, having to see to Maria before she had her own breakfast. It was still too cold to open the tiny window so she tried to get rid of the rank smell by hanging up bags of lavender.

One morning, on her way up to Maria's room, she felt dizzy. She stopped and clutched the thin rail on the stairs before pulling herself up the remaining steps. On the last step her waters broke. She called down to her husband who rushed up and got her into bed. That was all he had time to do. After eight children, her body was so primed that the baby, yet another girl, almost shot out.

It wasn't the first time George had dealt with his wife's quick deliveries, yet he never ceased to be amazed and elated at the sight of another tiny, dark-haired girl. Jane was allowed in to watch and help with the umbilical cord. She did her best to clean up the mess. Susanna lay back on the bed, also a little surprised by the speed of it all. Then she remembered her mother-in-law. She'd been on her way to see to her.

141

'George – leave the baby now,' she ordered. 'Go and see to your mother. Jane can finish cleaning up.' He passed her the baby to see if she would suckle. 'And get Cecilia to fetch Sarah Ezard. She'll see I'm all right.'

George returned almost immediately from his mother's room and knelt beside the bed. He held Susanna's hand then buried his face into the cover and burst into tears. She guessed that his mother had died. Maria could not have gone on for much longer. She stroked his hair, guilty that all she felt was relief. As they waited for Sarah Ezard, they heard John in the next room reading Maria's favourite Bible passage to her, one last time.

'To every thing there is a season, and a time to every purpose under the heaven: A time to be born, and a time to die.'

'We'll call the baby Mary,' Susanna murmured as she kissed the top of George's head. 'She'll be in remembrance of your mother.' She prayed that George would find some comfort from this. She also prayed that this baby girl really would be her last.

Chapter 26

Mary hoped it would be third time lucky with her next child. As the witch bottle under the hearth had not averted ill fortune so far, she tried other ways. She got out an old pair of shoes that had been her favourite years ago and sniffed them. They should work well, she thought, as they still carried a smell. They'd act as a spirit trap and tempt any evil around the place to collect in them and leave her alone. She spat on them for extra protection and hid one up the chimney and one under the thatch. Then she made William carve a witch mark on the wooden beam in the kitchen. Reluctantly, he carved the capitals M and V joined together – an invocation to the Virgin Mary. It was all too papist and superstitious for him but, standing back, he could see they made a W for his name. Kate had another idea and, when she was alone with Mary, whispered it in case evil spirits overheard.

'Maybe a witch 'as cast a spell an' we need to remove it. I know 'ow to do it. I've seen me gran'mother try it.'

'Did it work though?'

'Don't know for sure. I left 'ome. Came to work i' Reighton.'

'All right,' agreed Mary. 'I'll try anything. What do we have to do?'

'I need some o' tha water – scaldin' 'ot.' Mary raised her eyebrows. 'Aye, an' then we'll put it in a pot wi' three nails an' some pins an' a bit o' salt. We keep it warm. Then stick pot i' fire embers for nine days an' nights. Never let it go cold.'

'William won't like it.'

'Don't tell 'im. I shan't say nowt. See – pot is like witch's bladder. Nails an' pins'll torment 'er somthin' rotten when she passes water. After a few days she'll remove 'er spell.'

Mary shivered and took a deep breath. She'd go to any lengths to have a baby thrive.

'All right, let's do it.'

When the weather turned warmer, Mary shared the village's sense of relief as the cattle were taken back out to feed on the new grass in the pasture. She became more hopeful though the memory of the two lost children remained – a pale grey shadow that hovered behind as if attached like a hood. When May Day arrived, she spent the day at her sister's house. Now seven months pregnant, she didn't feel like dancing, and Robert had forbidden Elizabeth to take part in unholy entertainments.

The Gurwood girls took full advantage of the festivities. They put on clean white stockings and decorated their gowns with flowers and green, pink and yellow ribbons. Anna Jordan walked with them to the field behind the church and thought it was now or never with John Gurwood. She'd never look better than this. Jane and Cecilia did their best to make sure John saw plenty of her. Despite their efforts, he still hankered only after Susan Jordan and was seen showing off to her in the churchyard, playing his fiddle as fast as possible. Anna saw him and lost heart; she wished she'd not made such an effort with her appearance. She had no choice but to carry on and pretend she was happy so, when the other girls met up to decorate the Maypole, she joined in. They'd all brought coloured ribbons and began to wind them round the birch pole.

While the girls were occupied, the lads started on the ale. Older folk brought food and drink but soon went home, content to leave the day to the youngsters. The afternoon passed pleasantly enough with singing and dancing but, by evening, groups of drunken lads were staggering about shouting and swearing. Anyone still sober made excuses to leave and go home. Susanna Gurwood made sure her daughters and Anna left before any fights started. John stayed longer since he was required as fiddler, and so had the opportunity to walk Susan Jordan home.

He found everything about Susan neat and pretty. She had black arched eyebrows and long eye lashes above a tiny nose. He was thinking of asking her father if he could begin to court her formally but, as they were both only nineteen, thought he'd better wait. On May Day, however, anyone was free to put an arm round a waist and try for a few kisses. Anna Jordan did not see them sneak behind the church, or see the smile of victory on Susan's face when John told her how lovely she was.

Susan was quite aware of her charms and allowed him to kiss her on the cheek. He wanted her mouth but she wriggled free and laughed. She didn't particularly care for him but was excited and flattered. She'd already enticed Simeon and was very disappointed when he'd left to live and work at Bartindale. Choice was limited. The other unmarried men, who weren't related, were either ugly or boring or both. There was always Tom, the hired lad at Uphall, but he unnerved her; she had the feeling he knew what she was really like. Also, he was friends with Anna Jordan, her rival over John Gurwood. As Susan said goodnight to John, she wondered if Simeon would ever come back to Reighton; until he did, she'd make do with John.

Stinky Skate still came to the village once or twice a month, depending on how much fish he had to sell. He always ambled along at the same pace which earned him another nickname – One-Speed-Stinky. With the warmer weather came other pedlars.

A woman called Speckledy Golightly arrived, though this wasn't her real name. She had a Scottish accent, carrot-coloured hair and a face full of freckles. Even her arms and hands were covered in brown spots as people noticed when she held out her ribbons for sale. She also sold pins and needles, threads, muslin, and woollen stockings. In late summer, after harvest, she bought plaited straw off the village girls and made it into hats. Depending on the season, she made brooms, brushes and baskets from heather stems.

She often had a feeling that folk were wary of her because of her accent.

Martha Wrench stood by the forge and grumbled to passers-by. 'Scotland may well be united with us now, but I bet she's a papist, an' a Jacobite spy an' all.'

Sarah Ezard felt only compassion when she saw the pedlar entering the village with a stooped back and one foot dragging behind.

'I bet she was quite 'andsome when she were younger,' she told the women as they fetched water from the well. They had to agree her face had good bone structure and her cheek bones carried a healthy flush. 'She's probably not as old as she looks,' added Sarah. 'She's just 'ad an 'arder life than most.'

No one bothered to find out about her past, not until her visits coincided with those of Stinky Skate. He'd been a widower for years and lived an independent life. It was he who teased out her story. He likened the process to pulling a loose tooth; it would seem to come free but then tighten and come no further then, with some guile, it could be pulled some more.

That summer he learned of the violent marriage that had forced her to run away from Glasgow. She spent years wandering the north of England as a leech finder, her bones and joints wrecked by the numbing waters of the black moorland pools. She waded barefoot in the soft, dark mud till it oozed between her toes and waited for leeches to attach themselves. Then she put them in a keg of water hung about her neck, her hands fumbling with the cold. Once back on dry land, the freezing winds slapped her bare, wet legs already red and raw from the icy water. After years of this hard existence, when her health was almost ruined, she gave it up to try her hand at being a pedlar. The long, cold winters brought her ever further south until she was now wandering between York and the coast.

Stinky Skate admired her patience and fortitude. His life, by contrast, had been easy and comfortable. He helped her by pointing out the different hamlets and the tracks to follow and offered her a roof over her head in Filey whenever she needed. She never minded his fishy smell, being only too glad of a friend. Soon, her freckled face was a familiar sight between Filey and Bridlington and she began to spend more time in and around Hunmanby and Reighton.

She was on her way to Hunmanby one day in June when she saw Mary standing outside her cottage door. Mary was eight months pregnant and feeling oppressed by the humid weather. Speckledy Golightly limped by and noticed Mary take deep breaths and rub her back. As she passed, the pedlar asked Mary if there was anything she needed.

'No thank you, not today,' Mary answered, watching the woman hobble away. Then she changed her mind. 'Wait! Come back!' she shouted. When the woman returned, Mary spoke quietly in case anyone overheard. 'I wonder if you have something for childbirth … well, not for the birth exactly, but … I don't know … something.'

'What ails thee, lassie?'

'Nothing. I'm in good health, but …' Mary didn't want to talk out in the lane so asked the pedlar in and, sitting across the kitchen table, told her all about little Thomas and the lost daughter. Speckledy Golightly listened without interrupting and then reached down into her basket and rummaged about under the stockings. Mary craned her neck to peep, but the wily woman turned her back. Mary had heard of the existence of a special penny that worked like a charm. She knew of farmers who'd used it to get rid of cattle disease or change their luck at harvest time. Speckledy Golightly held up a coin and told Mary that, if she drank water that had been stirred with this coin, good luck would follow.

'How much will you charge?'

'Nae worry, lassie. Nae worry. When I see thee with a healthy wee bairn, I'll take some eggs in exchange.'

Mary thanked her and did as she was told.

In early July, she gave birth to a healthy boy. As she looked at him crying with gusto, she hardly dared to hope.

Chapter 27

1707-8

The new baby was baptised Francis, after his grandfather. Mary thought this unfortunate as the name reminded her of William's bullying brother. She had little choice in the matter as the previous babies had been named after her own family. While the baby was healthy, she hadn't been well since the birth. She suffered days with a splitting headache and was so tired. Even her hair felt lifeless and had lost its shine. No one, not even Kate, took her seriously. You were expected to be exhausted after giving birth. The weather didn't help. It was a hot summer and the house was like an oven. Mary longed to open the windows and feel a breeze but knew she couldn't because of the baby.

'After tha churchin' tha'll be fine,' said William's mother, but the day of the churching came and went and Mary still wasn't herself. William couldn't understand her. The baby was fine, Mary's milk was coming through in abundance and she should have been happy. Instead, she was uneasy and worried that the hot weather would lead to fevers, that this latest child might also be taken. No matter how she tried, she couldn't relax and love the new baby in the same way as the others. She just did what she had to do, and the baby fattened and grew despite the lack of interest. William's mother was having none of it.

'She's be'avin' like a sullen, spoilt bairn,' she told him. 'Tha needs to get 'er be'avin' like a proper mother.'

He took the easier way out and ignored Mary's moods. Kate also ignored Mary most of the time and just hoped the miserable time would pass.

It wasn't until the harvest was safely in that Mary began to revive. She still grieved for the children she'd lost, but now began to feel sorry for the new baby boy; he was innocent and didn't deserve to be treated so coldly by his own mother. She now took him off Kate more often and even spent time playing with him. The baby, in turn, responded more to his mother but maintained a strong affection for Kate, continuing, once fed, to seek her rather than his mother for comfort.

As Mary and William enjoyed sleeping together once more, their relationship improved. Mary recalled Speckledy Golightly and the coin she'd been given. Lying on her back in bed one night, content at last with her life, she wondered if it was that which had changed their luck.

William also appreciated the change in fortune. One evening as he walked home in late autumn, the sun was still ablaze in the sky, setting in such a glorious way that it was good to be alive. He was aroused by the thought of Mary waiting for him with a hot supper and, he hoped, an early night. The hawthorn hedges along St Helen's Lane were flecked with gold from the sun, blinding him as he walked westwards. His breeches were warm against his thighs and he thought more of that early bedtime. Married life was a fine thing. He wished he'd wedded earlier, not left it so long, not suffered quite so long on his own getting tense and frustrated. Happy in his lot, he looked forward to the coming winter, and long nights with Mary.

Others were not so happy. The vicar, for one, was disturbed by events in the north. He knew the Act of Union had caused discontent in parts of Scotland.

'There've been food riots up in the northeast,' he told his son one quiet winter's evening. The women of the house had all retired to bed leaving the two men in the kitchen to enjoy their last pipe of the day by the dying fire. As he tamped down the tobacco he pursed his lips. 'You know, John, I do believe the Scots think we've bankrupted them.'

'The union with us must have been the last straw then.' John sucked on his pipe, sending whiffs of smoke from the side of his mouth. He coughed as he added, 'I can't see how they can really expect to get their own king back.'

'That'll never happen! There's not a chance we'll allow a Catholic king. Not a chance!' The vicar burnt his thumb as he prodded down the smouldering tobacco. 'God damn them. I can't think straight.' He was defiant as he pushed in more tobacco. 'From now on it's going to be the subject of my sermons. We're Anglicans and we're going to stay that way. No papists are going to disturb *our* way of life.' Roused by the conversation, they finished their pipes much quicker than usual and retired to bed still grumbling about the Scots.

True to his word, George Gurwood delivered some strong sermons and anti-Catholic sentiment ran high. As a result, when Speckledy Golightly entered the village she was shunned.

'There's no 'arm in 'er,' pleaded old Ben. 'She's only a poor lass tryin' to make a livin' like rest of us.' In their hearts many knew this was true, yet no one wanted to be seen talking to a Scot or buying from her. She would have starved if it hadn't been for Stinky Skate. He took her back with him to Filey where she laid low for a while, waiting for times to change. Mary felt guilty about turning her back on the pedlar who'd been so kind, so she gave Stinky Skate money to buy sewing items. If only she knew, half the village was doing the same. Speckledy Golightly managed to get through the year, thanks to the secret trading.

Others in Reighton were also affected by national events beyond their control. The following April, eligible men in the area wondered whose name would be picked out for military service. No one wanted to do it. William and the other yeomen knew they could afford to pay for a substitute, but it was a tenant farmer, Henry Vesey, who was called up. The man cursed his luck and marched straight to the forge to vent his anger.

'I'm a widower,' he complained, 'and I've just the one son. 'Ow is 'e supposed to manage on 'is own?'

The blacksmith carried on filing a bolt. 'Can't tha rake up the ten pounds for someone else to do it?' he asked.

'No.' Henry Vesey turned and marched out, kicking over an empty bucket as he left.

Weeks later, Henry was back at the forge, a much happier man. 'I don't know why I was so worried,' he said. 'Tha should see 'em. That militia – they don't know what they're doin'. All I've 'ad to do is a few days of drill.' He chuckled to himself. 'Tha wouldn't believe the way them officers fiddle an' faddle about – they couldn't train a dog. Daft as dormice the lot of 'em. I bet none of 'em 'as seen any real service.'

The blacksmith tried to dampen Henry's mood. 'If the war goes badly then tha'll 'ave to go.'

'True, but I reckon I'd only be sent as far as Bridlington garrison. I'd relieve one o' their regulars an' be safe there.' Undaunted, Henry Vesey strode away, avoiding any buckets.

News came through in the summer that a Jacobite rising had failed. In August, just before harvest time, George Gurwood read out the prescribed prayer issued to all the Anglican churches.

'We give hearty thanks for the happy success of her Majesty's councils and forces against the late insolent and unjust attempt of the common enemy and the Pretender, to invade her Majesty's kingdom of Great Britain; as also for the late great victory obtained over the French army near Audenarde.'

He explained to his congregation how the French had supported the Jacobite cause and had sailed to Scotland. 'I am informed that the French sent thirty ships with six thousand men.' He waited while the enormity of this sank in and then smiled. 'We can thank the Lord for his mercy – they took too long to get here and our Royal Navy was waiting for them.' He enjoyed relaying news of the French humiliation and laughed. 'It says something about the French – they refused to even land James the Pretender and, instead, turned tail and set off immediately back to France.'

There was some laughter in the church and a few jeers. Henry Vesey was so pleased he stood up and thrust his fist in the air in triumph.

'Yes,' George added with another smile, 'the rebellion has been a pitiful failure.'

The Scots were now a laughing stock. Speckledy Golightly had suffered worse and could live with that.

William's brother, Francis, though living and working at Argam, had got into the habit of attending church in Reighton on Sundays. It gave him the chance to visit his mother and catch up on any news. Simeon also went to Reighton church but with different intentions. He swaggered past Susan Jordan fully aware of the effect of his physique. Tall, with broad shoulders, a narrow waist, a flat stomach and firm thighs, he knew John Gurwood was no competition.

Susan's heart beat faster as soon as she knew of Simeon's presence in the church. When he glanced her way his dark eyes seemed to bore into her so that she became confused and had to look away. She knew he could be cruel but wanted him anyway. He was dangerous yet exciting. Instead of listening to the sermon, she imagined walking along the cliffs with him at her side and the wind blowing in her hair. Each Sunday fed her desires and her daydreams grew bolder. She imagined herself being held by Simeon and kissed until she was out of breath. She daren't think further ahead – it was too disturbing while trying to sit prim and upright in a church pew. Her sister, Isabella, always nudged her and told her to stop fidgeting.

Simeon knew his long glances were having an effect and, with past experience, knew it wouldn't be long before he could make a move. John Gurwood remained unaware of the smouldering passions developing a few pews behind him. Susan still walked out with him regularly and often allowed him a kiss on the cheek. Once she'd even let him kiss her on the lips. She did it to imagine Simeon's mouth on hers.

Anna Jordan, also in church each Sunday, only had eyes for John Gurwood. She'd watch him and stare at the back of his Sunday wig, absorbing every little detail as if her life depended on it. She feasted her eyes on the bottle-green velvet bow on his plait, the turn of his neck and the way he stood up to sing the hymns. Her daydreams were of marriage and a home together, bearing his children and sharing a life with the Gurwood family. Whenever she prayed, his name was mentioned. She loved him and believed that, in time, he would come to love her too.

Everyone in the village knew her fondness for him.

Sarah Ezard, sitting with Ben at the back of the church, elbowed him and pointed at Anna. 'Look – she's oglin' John again. She'd make 'im a lovely wife. She's kind an' thoughtful.'

'Aye,' said Ben, 'an' she's already well in wi' Gurwoods, a great friend to all them lasses.' They both agreed it would be a perfect match.

John hadn't the sense to see it and, the more people and his sisters sang Anna's praises, the more he turned a deaf ear.

Chapter 28

1708

In August, William and his father spent days ruminating over the state of the grain. The cold spring and the variable summer meant the corn was stunted. The harvest would be meagre so it was essential to reap at just the right time and not let any go to waste. One Saturday they picked more samples of wheat and rolled them around their palms to see if they were light and dry enough. The grain was ripe and, coupled with what looked to be a spell of dry weather, they wanted no delay. George Gurwood duly announced in church that the harvest would begin and the whole village prepared to start the next day. Francis and Simeon were asked to stay over at Uphall to help.

After the service, John Gurwood walked Susan home, as usual. When he left he didn't notice Simeon lurking at the side of the house. Susan had seen him and her heart leapt. When the coast was clear, Simeon knocked on her door. She answered it and feigned surprise. He took off his hat and looked her straight in the eye.

'I was wonderin' if tha'd like a walk later.'

'Nay, I can't,' she heard herself say, as if it was someone else speaking, 'I'm 'elpin' Isabella i' kitchen.' Damn the kitchen, she thought.

'Well then,' he replied softly, 'there's other days. I'll be at 'arvest wi' rest of 'em. I'll be 'ere till 'arvest is over.' He gave her a knowing look as he replaced his hat, and then stood unmoving, gazing into her eyes until she closed the door on him. She leant her back against the wall and breathed deeply to calm herself, but her legs were shaking as she walked back to the kitchen. Simeon, as he made his way back to Uphall, was reckoning on how many days it would take to harvest the wheat and have his way with Susan.

Next morning everyone gathered at Uphall in the early sunshine to be allotted their tasks. Francis Jordan hardly needed to organise the women; they knew who worked well together. With their sharpened sickles held under their arms, they looked like an invading army. They stood around the yard in groups of six, each team waiting eagerly for Francis to allocate a man to bind their wheat. Mary left her young son with her mother so she could join Anna and Kate once more and be part of the best get-together in the farming year. As soon as the men knew who they were with, the teasing and joking began. They were only silenced when George Gurwood appeared with his family to lead the procession to the wheat field. Mary saw John Gurwood wink at Susan. She hoped Anna had not noticed.

They all followed the vicar up the hill to the southernmost field. George, in his gown and carrying the Bible, was followed closely by the Jordans. The Gurwood girls had twined flowers into their hair and the youngest ones skipped and ran to keep up. Once they reached the field, John Gurwood held the Bible while his father read out verses from Psalm 65. With both arms raised to the cloudless sky, the vicar read out in a loud voice so that all could hear.

'Thou visitest the earth, and waterest it: thou greatly enriches it with the river of God, which is full of water: thou preparest them corn, when thou hast so provided for it … Thou crownest the year with thy goodness; and thy paths drop fatness. Thanks be to God. Amen.'

They echoed the Amen and then George Gurwood took up Mary's sickle. With great ceremony, he cut the first corn. A cheer went up and the women trooped forward to their places to begin cropping the wheat. The youngest teams showed off and worked at a fast rate but soon tired and settled down to a more sensible pace. As the wheat was short and uneven in its growth, it made the reaping that much harder, but soon everyone was working with a steady rhythm.

The women faced the corn with the sun and the southern breeze behind them and, before long, their backs and arms were wet with sweat. Dust from the dry grain settled into their hair despite their bonnets and worked its way into the creases of their elbows making sore, red lines. Their eyes smarted and their backs ached. All day they worked at a measured pace, enjoying short breaks for a drink while keeping an eye on the sky for clouds.

Over the next few days the breeze grew stronger as it veered to the east and then turned north-easterly. The sky clouded over and the sea turned brown with huge, rolling waves. Francis Jordan was relieved when the rain held off and the strong wind helped to dry the sheaves. When the last part of the field was cut, the weather stayed sunny the whole day. Everyone was tanned wherever the sun reached their skin. The boys and men had white necks where their kerchiefs had been, but their arms, up to their rolled-up sleeves, were brown as nuts.

The children sensed the end of the harvest and began to play about. Tom lost control over Richard and Samuel Jordan and just let them chase around the stooks. John and Jane Gurwood had also given up the battle with their young sisters who now sat in the shade of a stook with Cecilia, learning how to plait straws.

Only the very middle of the field was left to cut. The men waded in and the rats and mice that had taken refuge among the last corn stalks bolted for cover. Dickon set loose the dogs. The rats were seized, shaken, or tossed into the air. The vermin did not stand a chance. The children cheered when Francis Jordan shot a lone rabbit as it raced for the hedge. It was now the end of the wheat harvest proper and a time to have fun. Mary laid down her sickle, wondering who would be chosen to cut the very last stalks.

'Who's goin' to cut yon Old Witch down?' Dickon shouted. The women looked at each other, wondering who Francis Jordan would pick.

'Mary!' he shouted. 'Thoo's a mother now. Thoo'd best 'ave a go.' Everyone gathered round to watch.

'Cut Old Witch! Cut Old Witch!' they chanted as Mary sliced through the last of the standing corn. William bent down to make it into a small sheaf and bind it.

'Burn Old Witch! Burn Old Witch!' everyone shouted, and the children began fetching brushwood to heap up for the fire. Young Richard Jordan had already chosen Margaret Gurwood as his dancing partner and both five-year-olds hopped and danced around the growing pile. When it was high enough, William placed the last sheaf on top.

'There you go, you Old Witch,' he said. 'Burn well.' He took hold of Mary's hand and kissed her on the cheek. As his father bent down to light the fire, William faced the crowd and shouted, 'Where's John Gurwood? John – run an' get tha fiddle.'

As the flames leapt through the dry wood and gorse, catching the last sheaf, John rushed away down the hill. Anna Jordan watched him till he was out of sight, then went with the Gurwood girls and Tom to fetch the sled piled high with pea reaps and kegs of ale. Tom tossed the dry pea plants onto the fire and everyone settled down to drink and wait for the pods to cook and burst open.

All eyes were on the fire, and Simeon saw his chance. No one saw him sidle up to Susan and whisper in her ear. His hot breath caught her off-guard. Had she heard right? Did he want to meet her that night? She spun round to face him and their cheeks brushed together.

'Aye,' she whispered. He pressed a kiss on her lips and her body lurched. That never happened when John kissed her. They moved apart and Simeon went to rejoin the men.

When John returned with his fiddle, everyone cheered and began to make up ridiculous drinking toasts. Robert Storey pulled Elizabeth to one side.

'It's time we went,' he said. 'They're going to be drinking more than is good for them.' Mary saw Elizabeth hesitate and then give in. She was sorry to see her sister leave so early and miss the fun. While Robert escorted his wife from the field, John played the traditional Harvest Home tune. They all sang as they drank toasts to the lasses and lads, to the sickle, the scythe and the plough, even to the pails and the flails.

As soon as the song was over, John sat down next to Susan to enjoy the roasted peas. Her face was flushed by the fire and her eyes glistened. He persuaded her to see him that night; he planned to tell her how much she meant to him. She decided that, when he called for her, Isabella could tell him she'd already gone to meet him. That way she could avoid him and see Simeon instead. Full of confidence and looking forward to the evening, she told John to play his fiddle again and got up to dance. Others followed her example. They danced round the fire, some of the young men leaping right over it.

As more ale was drunk and the sun began to set, the older women dragged their children away. Mary and William joined them to go and collect their son. With reluctance they left the field, stopping now and again to look back at the dying fire and the dancers. The older men also left the field; they were tired but relaxed and just wanted to rest and put their feet up at home.

Anna stayed with the other single young men and women. As John played his fiddle ever faster, Susan danced as if possessed. She had so much more energy than anyone else. All eyes were drawn to her. When the fire died down, she was the first to rub her hands in the ashes and race after her brothers. She blackened their faces and then raced after John Jordan. Francis and Simeon made a fuss and complained loudly that she hadn't blackened them yet, but she just laughed and ran to blacken John Gurwood's face instead. Anna looked on. John had a ridiculous grin on his face.

Eventually, with the fire out, and the ale kegs empty, it began to grow cold. The sun had set and a full moon was rising above the sea. Simeon boasted to Francis that he was meeting Susan later on at the north side of the church. Francis knew that John had also arranged to see Susan. He had a plan at last to get his own back on his sister Anna. As they all staggered back home he caught up with her, took her arm in his, and whispered what she'd always wanted to hear.

'I've a message for you – from John.' She stopped breathing. 'He wants to meet with you tonight. Be at the church wall on the north side in an hour.' Her head was spinning. She could hardly believe it. John did want her after all.

Chapter 29

1708

When Anna walked down the hill she'd never felt so alive, neither had the night sky ever looked such a beautiful deep blue. Tom was walking just behind her and wondered what on earth Francis had said to make her so distracted. He wanted to tell her how much he liked her and thought John must be mad to prefer Susan. Simeon had walked on ahead, keen to get to Uphall and wash off the harvest dust. John Gurwood walked beside Susan and Isabella, helping guide her brothers who lurched and stumbled, much the worse for drink.

At home, and with the door closed behind them, Susan whispered to her sister that, instead of going straight to bed, she'd have a wash and then go for a short walk with John. Isabella wasn't surprised and told her not to be late back. Father was frail and already in bed – he wouldn't want to worry or be disturbed. The two brothers had already collapsed senseless onto their bed. Alone in the kitchen, Susan paced up and down. The more she watched the candle, the slower it seemed to burn. When at last the candle had burnt an hour, she slipped out of the back door and headed for the church.

Simeon was already there waiting. He leant casually against the north wall, gazing   out over the moonlit bay feeling rather pleased with himself.

At Uphall, Anna had washed and then pretended to go to bed. Her parents assumed that she was asleep with her two sisters, but an hour later she whispered, full of excitement, that she was meeting John at the church. Dorothy, who was only fifteen, was amazed. Harvests and full moons certainly had a powerful effect. Jane just yawned.

'Give him a kiss for me,' she murmured and then rolled over and fell asleep once more. Anna gave Dorothy a kiss, not quite knowing why – she just felt so much love for everyone that night. She also hugged her before she left.

'Don't stay awake for me,' she said. 'You know I'll be safe with John. Wish me luck.'

At the vicarage, John Gurwood's parents didn't hear him creep downstairs. The house was dark and silent. As he passed through the parlour, he bumped into the end of the girls' bed. It awoke Jane who asked if he was ill. He knelt down beside her and whispered that he'd arranged to see Susan.

'It's for a short, moonlit walk – nothing else, I promise. I won't be long. Go back to sleep.' When Jane sighed he added, 'I am twenty years old – it's time I thought of getting married.'

'Go on then,' she said wearily. He was never going to choose Anna. 'Do whatever you like. I don't care.'

'Fine,' he replied. 'I'll be on my way then. Goodnight.'

She heard him lift the latch and close the door gently behind him. Left alone with all her sisters, she wondered how long it would be before someone was attracted to her. She fell asleep thinking of a possible future with a bed just to herself and a husband.

John controlled the urge to run as he walked down the hill to Susan's house. On arriving, he gave his usual three taps on the door. When no one came he wondered if she'd decided to walk on ahead. They had a favourite stroll that took them by the church with a good view of the bay so he set off back the way he'd come. He hadn't gone far when he saw two figures by the north wall. At first he couldn't see who it was so crept closer. They never saw him. They were far too engrossed to notice anything. He realised with horror that it was Susan and Simeon.

At first he couldn't move. His legs were locked as if made of wood. There was a thudding in his chest and a strange blocked-up feeling in his ears. He grabbed the churchyard wall to steady himself. Not knowing what to do, he staggered further up the hill to the church gate. He needed to keep walking – anywhere, in the cool night air. As he strode blindly through the churchyard and out the other side towards the hills and the sea, he missed seeing Anna Jordan who had just reached the north wall of the church.

She rounded the corner and saw the back of Susan Jordan kissing someone. She thought it was John Gurwood. They were so engrossed they were quite unaware of her presence. In a daze, she backed off. She couldn't believe that John could be so fickle. Why had he wanted to meet her if he was still in love with Susan? It didn't make any sense at all. She felt sick. Unable to face returning home, she walked through the churchyard and headed east to the cliff tops going in the same direction as John.

She stopped when she reached Knox Well. The stones round the edge shone in the moonlight and, for a moment, she considered throwing herself down it. Instead, she sat on the rim and cried. The moon was shining over Filey Bay, the moon that would have been so perfect if she'd been with John. It was all too late for her now. She'd have preferred a dark night, black as her mood. The cold stone of the well seeped through her cloak and made her shiver. Suddenly she sprang up, grabbed a loose stone and threw it as hard as she could at the moon. Then, her eyes blurred with tears, she ran on towards the sea.

She snaked her way between the clumps of gorse, not caring how often she snagged her cloak. Finally, she reached the cliff top. Standing still on the edge, she could hear the tide receding. The salty sea air blew fresh and cold against her tear-stained cheeks. She shivered again and pulled her cloak closer. It was then that she saw someone in the distance striding along the cliff northwards to Hunmanby Gap. It was John Gurwood. She recognised his walk. So it couldn't have been him with Susan. She called out to him. If he heard her he did not acknowledge it but carried on walking.

She decided to try and catch up with him, every few minutes calling his name though the wind took her voice away. After a while she had to give up. The grass on the cliff top was wet and slippery with dew. It wasn't a safe place to be out walking on your own even on such a moonlit night. She stopped to get her breath back and gazed out over the sea where the moon was making such a bright silver pathway. She imagined herself walking along that cold, glittering trail. Near the horizon some cobles were fishing for mackerel. The lights from their lanterns glimmered as the swell lifted and dropped. Watching them and the moonlit sea, she breathed in time to the waves that lapped below. She was calm now, almost weightless.

John was far from this state; he was still seething with emotions he found impossible to handle. He strode well past Hunmanby Gap before he stopped. Then he also gazed out over the sea, but with such mixed feelings of anger, betrayal, jealousy, humiliation, self-pity, and then anger again followed by jealousy – always jealousy. It was driving him mad. He couldn't stand still. Recalling the sight of Susan with Simeon, he stamped about on the ground and kicked at the tufts of grass in his way. He grabbed his head with both hands and squeezed hard, just to feel a different pain. He thumped his legs as he stomped up and down cursing and not knowing where to walk to next.

At last his anger and some stubborn pride outweighed the jealousy and humiliation. He turned round and walked back along the cliff top, taking the short cut from Hunmanby Gap through the meadows and along Oxtrope Lane. He never saw Anna.

Chapter 30

1708

The next morning Francis and Simeon were up before dawn and returned to their farms before the others had even had breakfast. Francis knew better than to outstay his welcome; he was still unpopular with his father. He didn't know that Anna had not returned from her evening tryst. It was his sister Dorothy who raised the alarm. The youngsters couldn't understand why Anna wasn't there. She was more like a mother than a sister. She looked after them when they were ill. She sorted out their arguments and made sure the food servings were fair. They could not imagine life at Uphall without her. Neither could Tom. As soon as he realised her absence he questioned everyone. In the end Dorothy confessed that Anna had been going to meet John Gurwood at the church. When her father found out he went straight to the vicarage and banged his fist on the door.

Most of the Gurwood family were still getting dressed. George Gurwood answered the door himself to find an angry, red-faced Francis Jordan standing there, out of breath. He didn't even get the chance to ask what was wrong.

'Where's John? Where is 'e? Eh?' demanded Francis. 'I want to know what 'e's done with Anna.' In his anxiety he forgot where he was and tried to push past the vicar.

George held him back. 'Now you just wait, Francis! I don't know what you're talking about.'

'Then I'll tell thee. That son o' thine 'as taken our Anna. God knows what 'e's done with 'er. She 'asn't come 'ome. Been out all night, poor lass. Where's John? Ask 'im. Fetch 'im 'ere. I want to 'ave words with 'im.'

'I think you're mistaken,' replied the vicar but, seeing Francis in such a wild state, he decided he'd better placate him. 'Come on in, Francis,' he said gently, 'we'll sort this out. Come and sit in the kitchen. I'll get John up and we'll ... we'll sort it out, I'm sure.'

Everyone in the house, except for John, had heard the raised voices. He was still fast asleep after his long, frantic night. When he was woken roughly, it took him only a moment to remember his misery. Suddenly empty and drained of life, he had no idea why his father was staring at him and still shaking him.

'Did you go out last night?' his father asked. John didn't answer. 'John! It's important. Did you go out last night?' Still he didn't answer but looked confused and rubbed his eyes. 'John! Get up. Get dressed. There's Francis Jordan downstairs. He's saying you were with Anna last night.'

'Well, I wasn't,' he answered sullenly, and got out of bed to get dressed.

'Do you know anything about Anna?'

'No. I don't care about Anna. I'm sick of hearing about Anna.'

George Gurwood wanted to hit him. He gritted his teeth. 'There's Anna's father,' he said, 'he's beside himself with worry. Anna didn't come home last night. He seems to think she was with you. Now why would he think that? John?'

'I don't know. I don't know. I went out to meet Susan.' He left it there, unwilling to say more and recall the horror of the evening. His father believed him. Together they went downstairs to explain.

Francis looked like a broken man. He was sitting on a stool in the kitchen bending his hat every way possible. He leapt up as soon as he saw John. George stepped quickly between them to avoid violence.

'It wasn't John she was with; he was with Susan.'

John looked sheepish at this point. What he'd said wasn't exactly true and he was afraid the whole village would get to know how Susan had made a fool of him. Still, he was at a loss to know why there was a fuss over Anna.

Francis eyed John up, knowing there was more to it, and then spoke slowly, emphasising every word as if talking to a simpleton.

'My Dorothy told me this mornin' that Anna said she were meetin' thee. Now why would she say that, eh? Is thoo sayin' my daughter's a liar?'

'Now, you can just stop there, Francis,' interrupted George. 'I believe my son when he says he was with Susan.'

'Then it's a damn mystery,' shouted Francis, and then mumbled to himself. 'But where's Anna? Who can tell where she is?' He collapsed back down onto the stool and began to cry. 'I can't go back to Up'all without knowin' summat. I can't.' They took pity on him and said they'd go back with him and help look for Anna.

At Uphall, Tom was trying to organise search parties. Dickon offered to do his morning chores for him. Luckily, the stooks were still drying in the field so everyone had spare time. When Francis returned with the vicar and his son, small groups set out to search the Reighton area. Tom even made sure that a group went towards Argam and another towards Bartindale; he couldn't help suspecting that Francis or Simeon might have something to do with Anna's sudden disappearance. If only John *had* been with Anna, then she'd have been home again and happy. He didn't care anymore if she loved John instead of him; he just wanted her to be safe.

Tom chose to search the hill behind the church. Accompanied by Robert Storey and William, he walked round each clump of gorse. He got his hopes up when threads from Anna's red, woollen cloak were found caught on the thorns. They searched every inch of the hill methodically but found no more trace of her.

Robert Storey reached the cliff first and looked down. The tide had gone out a little, and Anna's body, still in its red cloak, was stranded on the sand at the foot of the cliffs. He'd no doubt she was dead. Her face was buried in the wet sand with her tangled, chestnut hair spread out in a circle. He shouted and ran back towards Tom and William. They saw him waving and were suddenly hopeful.

'She's down on the sands,' Robert shouted. As they came closer he added, 'I'm sorry. I don't think she can be alive.'

Tom couldn't believe it and ran ahead to see for himself. When he reached the place and looked down, there could be no mistake. Her hair still looked so pretty next to the wet, red cloak. William reckoned they should go down by way of the ravine and somehow manage to carry her up, so they scrambled down between the cliffs. As soon as their feet touched the sand, Tom ran towards her and ripped off his jacket to cover her body. He glared at the others as they approached and shouted hoarsely.

'I'll carry 'er back. Leave me to do it.' William put an arm round him but was shrugged off. Tom fiddled with his jacket, tucking it round Anna.

Robert intervened. 'You can't manage by yourself, Tom. Come on, let us help.'

Tom wiped his eyes with his shirt sleeve. He wished he was alone with Anna but gave in and let them help lift her body out of the wet sand. He fumbled with her cloak and gown to make sure she was decent. She looked as if she was asleep but her face was unnaturally white and wet sand clung to her cheeks. As they set off back to the ravine, he put a fist to his mouth to stifle any sobs.

Anna was laid out in the parlour at Uphall. Sarah Ezard came to wash and prepare her for the mourners. Despite her long experience, she'd never been quite so affected by the sadness and futility of a death. Anna was only nineteen years old, with a fine, healthy body. She should have lived to be married and enjoy love and motherhood. Sarah did her work but stopped frequently to blow her nose.

Uphall was so quiet, as if everyone had stopped breathing. Even the chickens and pigs in the yard were subdued by the melancholy air around them. Only Anna's mother remained the same. She asked William to send Kate to help with the food preparation, knowing that most of the village would be visiting to pay their respects. She bustled about the kitchen, giving orders as if it was just another day.

'Don't mind Dorothy,' Sarah advised Kate. 'It's only 'er way of copin', keepin' 'erself occupied.'

George Gurwood was one of the first visitors and suggested that the funeral be on Sunday so that everyone could and would attend. He found Francis sitting alone in the parlour beside Anna. She was laid on a straightening board on the table. A candle had been placed in her hands across her breast and the Gurwood girls had arranged bunches of daisies and wild, white roses round her. Normally, George would suggest that his son play the fiddle for the wake on Saturday evening, but he was unsure how John would be welcomed so didn't dare mention it.

Certain villagers were already beginning to whisper among themselves about the 'mystery' of Anna's death. Jane Gurwood heard Isabella and Susan hinting at suicide; they implied John's rejection had proved too much. Jane thought it was bad enough to lose a close friend without having the extra worry that Anna may have committed such a sin. She hated to think of Anna being buried in a field somewhere in unconsecrated ground, rather than in her own churchyard. All afternoon she worried about it before approaching her father. He was in the parlour preparing his sermon and was annoyed to hear of the rumours.

'How well did you know Anna?' he asked. 'And how well do you know Isabella and Susan? Who do *you* think is most likely to sin?'

As Jane looked so upset he asked her to sit with him awhile. The others were out with their mother picking more flowers for the funeral. The house was unusually quiet. Jane wiped her eyes and he continued more gently.

'It's my belief – no, I'm certain – Anna had grace. Remember, it was always Anna who found a way to soothe people, to make them behave better. She'd never have given in to morbid feelings or self-pity. She was always so full of hope and looking to the future.'

Jane smiled at her father through fresh tears. It was some comfort to hear him say such things. If only John had seen half as much in Anna. She decided to confide in her father and told him about her brother's behaviour. He listened patiently but had little to add.

'Best leave John to himself for a while,' he replied. 'No doubt he has something on his conscience. He'll have to come to terms with himself in his own time.'

For the next two days John sat in his room, refusing to come for meals. His mother interrogated him about his whereabouts on Thursday night but got no more out of him. Anna's death remained a mystery.

Chapter 31

1708

On Saturday a stillness settled over Uphall. The birds continued to sing and the sheep bleated on the moor as usual, but no one did any work except for the essential care of the stock. At the vicarage the Gurwood girls spent most of the day making a maiden's crown to hang over the Jordans' pew after the funeral. They folded and crimped pieces of white paper to make tiny rosettes and fixed them on to a helmet-shaped willow frame. The youngest sisters were excited by the sudden activity accompanied by intense whisperings. They couldn't comprehend that Anna would never visit them again. Jane Gurwood made a paper hand to hang inside the frame and on it she inscribed Anna's name and age and the date of her death. Since she was about the same age as Anna, she knew she'd be the one to walk in front of the coffin, carrying the crown.

The wake was a very quiet, sombre affair. On the Saturday evening, only Anna's closest relatives shared the vigil. The Uphall parlour was rich with the smell of candle wax and the extra flowers brought in by the Gurwood girls. William and John sat in silence with their father, smoking their pipes and sipping ale. They couldn't think of anything to say. They each grieved in their own way and tried to fathom out how exactly she'd met her end.

Dickon, at home with his wife, Isabel, was also puzzled by events. He reckoned that Francis and Simeon might be at the bottom of it as Tom had already voiced his suspicions.

'That poor lad,' said Isabel. ''E's goin' to miss Anna.'

'Aye. 'E's walkin' about like 'e can't see nor feel owt. I love 'im like me own son.'

'Can't we 'elp some'ow?' she asked. Dickon shrugged. It was a hopeless situation. Then his wife had an idea. 'Why doesn't tha go to Up'all an' ask if Tom can take a turn at sittin' with Anna?' Dickon thought this was going above his station but, once his wife had an idea, she was like a terrier with a rat and would never let go.

Dickon arrived at Uphall clean and dressed as if all ready for the funeral. Although surprised, they could understand why he wanted to share the vigil especially when he asked if Tom could join them. So it was that Tom had the chance to spend some time with Anna. The two of them took over from the others and Dickon sat quietly, as usual. He leant forward staring at the floor, fiddling with his hat. He let Tom cry when the boy couldn't hold back his tears and turned away when Tom held Anna's hand.

The next morning, Francis and Simeon arrived in high spirits for the Sunday Service. The air was fresh after the evening's shower and the early mist was lifting. It looked as if it was going to be another sunny day. They'd heard about Anna's disappearance when they saw people searching, but they remained unaware of her death.

As they approached the church the bells began tolling in groups of six denoting the funeral of a young maid. The noise seemed incongruous on such a fine morning. Then they saw Jane Gurwood leading a procession and carrying a maiden's crown. They assumed it was one of the Gurwood girls that had died and were shocked when they saw it was William and John carrying the coffin. Tom and Dickon were also helping and the other Jordans followed behind. On finding out that it was Anna who'd died, they joined the back of the procession, Francis now quite nervous and wondering how much he was to blame.

George Gurwood met them all at the church gate and led the way up the path. The whole of the village trooped into church and sat in their various pews. After placing the coffin at the front, Tom went to join the other hired lads at the back where they sat on benches. Dorothy Jordan caught his arm as he walked past. She motioned to him to join them in the Jordan pew. Such a precedent did not go unnoticed. When Dickon overheard the whispers and saw people nudge each other he was angry on Tom's behalf. Tom was worth the lot of them put together.

Susan Jordan sat with her sister, Isabella, and her two brothers. She appeared quite untouched by events, more interested in seeing Simeon again. Dickon, sitting behind their pew, heard them discussing suicide. He had a vision of a rat's nest breeding sickness and disease that would spread through the village. He coughed loudly to let them know he'd overheard. Jane Gurwood glanced behind and couldn't forget their insinuations about the way Anna had died; they made this funeral so much harder to bear. No matter what her father said, doubts lingered.

As the bells continued tolling, Sarah Ezard took hold of Ben's hand. She wondered why it was often the loveliest and kindest people who were taken early. She looked around and guessed there were many in church who regretted not paying Anna more attention.

Matthew Smith sat with his head bowed. He realised too late that Anna would have made a good wife and he'd have been more than happy to have married a Jordan. He was wondering why he hadn't tried to court her. Perhaps she'd be alive now if he had.

John Gurwood had reached a turning point. When he saw Susan in church that morning his stomach lurched, but not with the usual craving. He saw her as if for the first time and, for once, in a cold clear light. All Susan cared for was her appearance and her conquests. She was a shallow flirt full of her own importance. He now realised how much better Anna had been. He recalled how she'd looked on May Day and how smug he'd been at the attention she gave him. He'd flattered himself then on having better fish to fry. It was too late now to appreciate her worth.

As George Gurwood began the service, Elizabeth Storey grabbed her husband's hand. Anna's untimely death was a sharp reminder of the fragility of life. Deeply sorry for the Jordan family and for Tom, she sought comfort from Robert's body as she pressed closer to him in the pew. He remained as rigid as ever, his eyes on the vicar.

Dorothy Jordan sat tight-lipped and bolt-upright, her eyes straight ahead, while those around her looked crumpled and close to breaking down. Her husband seemed to have shrunk; his shoulders were hunched and he didn't lift his eyes from the floor. He couldn't bring himself to believe that Anna would never be coming back home. Most of the congregation were subdued but resigned; they'd seen youngsters taken early before, and no doubt would see more.

The service began with a hymn of praise and then Psalm 90 was read out by Matthew Smith. Tied to the land as they were, it was apt to hear imagery about grass.

'In the morning it flourish, and groweth up; in the evening it is cut down, and withereth.'

George Gurwood read the fifteenth chapter of Saint Paul's first epistle to the Corinthians. They'd heard it many times, knowing it was meant to offer comfort and hope, that at the last trumpet, the dead would rise uncorrupted.

'Death is swallowed up in victory,' the vicar read out loudly. 'O death, where is thy sting? O grave, where is thy victory?'

Normally, George Gurwood would proceed to the graveside and complete the service for the burial of the dead but, it being a Sunday, he had the opportunity to deliver a sermon. He looked down upon the expectant congregation and felt the grief of Francis and Dorothy at losing their eldest daughter so suddenly. He'd spent all the previous evening thinking over what his own daughter, Jane, had told him. He now intended to allay any doubts about the manner of Anna's death and spoke to them as a friend.

'I want you all to square your shoulders and lift your heads. Lift them up high.' They looked surprised and squirmed on their seats. 'Yes, that's right, sit up straight. Don't think I don't feel your sorrow. I do but ...' He paused and swallowed painfully as his voice failed him. 'But,' he continued, 'I want you all now to form a picture of Anna in your minds – it should be a beautiful vision. You've all seen her dressed up on May Day, and enjoying the dancing after the harvest, seen her busy about the village, working all hours under the sun. She was like a mother to her younger brothers and sisters. I'm sure they're remembering now what fun she could be. She helped Tom and Dickon at Uphall and was a true friend to many.' He stopped to wipe his nose and then added quietly, 'My own family in particular will sorely miss her. We all will. That's understood.' He glanced at Susan and Isabella Jordan and suddenly raised his voice. 'But it's a sin if we have any doubts about Anna, about her rightful place in glory. Anna's life was short, yes, but it was virtuous. I dare anyone to say otherwise.'

He paused and looked over the whole congregation. Satisfied they were of one mind, he continued. 'Death will always be a mystery and what is done cannot be undone.' He turned to the Bible and opened it at one of the pages he'd chosen from the Book of Job.

'Although affliction cometh not forth of the dust,' he read, 'neither doth trouble spring out of the ground: Yet man is born unto trouble, as the sparks fly upward.' He turned to other chapters. 'Seeing his days are determined, the number of his months are with thee, thou hast appointed his bounds that he cannot pass … Behold, God is great, and we know him not, neither can the number of his years be searched out.' He closed the Bible and looked at them with tears in his eyes.

'We cannot question the will of our Lord. But what we can do is be grateful. We can praise the life that Anna led. We can find comfort in the certainty that Anna had a good soul, young and unblemished. Surely she'll find her place among the angels and be blessed for evermore.' He opened his arms to them and took a deep breath.

'On such a day as this, with the sun now high in the sky and a fresh wind blowing in from the sea, I want you all to feel God's mercy and goodness. Our lives here on earth are short and we must love each other while we can. Remember the greatest commandments; love the Lord, thy God, and thy neighbour as thyself.'

Only the close family and Dickon and Tom attended the final committal in the graveyard. The rest of the congregation gathered at Uphall to share the funeral spread – a long table laden with pastries, cold meats, pickles and cheeses. As they ate and drank, the vicar's words lingered in their minds and they made a conscious effort to be kind and see the good in others. Francis and Simeon mixed with everyone else and all seemed forgiven – for the time being at least.

Part Three

The Great Frost

Chapter 32

1708-9

The exceptionally cold autumn that followed reflected the mood of the village. Many were still in shock after Anna's death. Her young brothers, Richard and Samuel, were only children and in need of lots of attention so Tom tried to spend more time with them. He sensed they were as lost as he was and took them brambling and showed them how to make grass whistles. He sought extra work to keep busy and be among people. Dickon kept a close eye on him. He saw that Tom was working as hard as ever and was full of smiles when he was with the children, but his face looked very bleak at times, his lips often drawn tight and his eyes blank.

Preparations for winter went on as usual at Uphall but, without Anna, the other daughters found they had so much more to do. They spent hours bent over the trough rubbing salt into the beef and hams. They went up and down the ladder taking apples to store under the roof and spent whole days making conserves and pickles. Now their hands were rough and sore and their hair stank of smoke.

Out in the barn, the hired lads were kept busy getting straw for thatching repairs, and Dickon went out on the moor with the shepherd to check that the ram had serviced all the ewes. William and John finished the final ploughing of the fallow field and hoped for dry weather so they could start harrowing and then sow the winter wheat.

All through that chilly autumn, Simeon continued to see Susan. When John Gurwood ignored her completely, she was rather relieved. Her thoughts, from waking in the morning to falling asleep at night, were centred on Simeon, on his body, his voice, his loving words, the places they'd met secretly and their future meetings. Her brothers were concerned as they knew the likes of Simeon. Isabella was envious but more annoyed by her sister's selfishness and listless approach to household tasks. Life was passing Isabella by. All she did was look after her father and brothers and cook and mend for them while Susan rushed hither and thither, flushed with new love.

At the height of the affair, Simeon was walking over to Reighton two or three times a week. Sometimes he was so eager he ran all the way. If Susan's father had known about it he'd have kept her in, but no one told him. He was ailing and fretted about every little thing so was spared the details of Susan's carryings on. It was very difficult, almost impossible however, to have secret meetings in the village. No matter where Susan and Simeon went, some field worker or passer-by would see them. They tried all kinds of places but eventually, as their passion grew, they became careless. Soon they were the main target of gossip. Yet still no one told Susan's father.

Life, for others, quietened down in November when the mists descended and the trees shed their last few leaves. Flocks of geese flew over, heading south, and Reighton was hit by the first sharp frosts. At Uphall, Dorothy continued to keep everyone occupied, especially her husband who was still dazed by grief. She made sure that December was spent checking the farm tools and equipment, making repairs and sharpening axes and saws.

Phineas Wrench was kept busy at the forge making nails, which were always in demand, as well as the usual door hinges and chains. His forge was the best place to gather and gossip now that the weather was colder and there was less work to do. In the afternoons when it grew dark, the forge was more like an alehouse. The shed reeked of tobacco and drink as well as horse sweat, singed hair and hooves. The blacksmith's wife had added honey to flavour her strongest brew; it was old Ben's idea and the sweet-tasting ale was quite addictive. The mothers and wives all knew where their men folk would be if they were not home by dusk.

One particularly cold Sunday morning in December, Ben and Sarah Ezard sat huddled at the back of the freezing church. They whispered together, recalling the long winters of their youth. Sarah mentioned the terrible winter of 1683, one of the worst she'd known. Ben argued that it had been much worse the year he'd broken his leg.

'Tha remembers them thirteen drifty days, eh? When it snowed i' March for thirteen days without a stop? Most o' sheep froze to death that spring.'

'Aye,' Sarah replied, 'but what about that frost before Christmas in '83? We 'eard River Thames 'ad frozen all way up to London Bridge. Aye – an' kept frozen for months an' a foot deep of ice. I remember no one 'ere could get a spade through soil – ground were 'ard as any stone.'

Ben was not to be outdone. 'What about year Jane Jordan were born? It never thawed 'ere for six month. There were ice o' sands right up to waves. I'd never seen owt like it.' They dreaded the return of those winters of the late 1600s; years when they were cut off completely from the outside world and when heavy snow even fell in May.

William Jordan, watching his breath steaming above the pew, was also remembering those cold winters. He and most of his brothers and sisters had been born then. He'd spent long, dark days kept indoors for weeks at a time, bundled up in such thick clothes he could hardly move. Other memories were of a silent white world, the snow piled up outside the house, and small birds, frozen to death, dropping from the trees. He shuddered to think of it happening again. To those who had still not recovered from the shock of Anna's death, the winter of 1709 would be a severe test of their physical and mental reserves.

The really cold spell began on the evening of 5th January. That night the temperature plummeted dramatically and kept falling. Rabbits froze in their burrows, and pheasants lay dead in the hedgerows. The wind came from the northeast and, although Filey Brigg stood out distinctly one morning in the sunshine, all views were soon blotted out by a snowstorm. The sky became a dirty yellow and everything went quiet as if nature itself had shut down. The heavy fall of snow settled and stayed for over three weeks. Folk stayed indoors whenever possible and just hoped they had enough food and fuel to last them.

The great frost came at a bad time as it coincided with the start of the ploughing season. At Uphall the ploughs and harnesses were ready after the Yuletide break, but then suddenly the ground had frozen solid. George Gurwood worried that, if anyone died, they would not be able to get a pickaxe through the ground to bury them. There was nothing anyone could do but wait and hope.

William and Mary kept a good fire going with gorse and dried dung and, like many others, they moved the beds into the kitchen. They also brought in their chickens and pig. Their son, Francis, was very happy with this change in his otherwise quiet life and, having just learnt to walk, had fun chasing the chickens about.

Dickon and Tom blocked up any draughty holes and gaps in the byre and stable and covered the horses with cloths. Even so, when Tom fed the horses in the morning he found icicles hanging from their muzzles. When they checked the cattle each day, some were so badly affected by the cold they had to be slaughtered. The surviving ones huddled together in misery, and the milkmaids complained when the lukewarm milk in their buckets grew a skin of ice.

As the days turned into weeks everyone economised on lighting and fuel and went to bed early in a vain attempt to keep warm. Elizabeth Storey had been enjoying the early nights. She'd still not quite given up hope of having a child. But Robert complained he wasn't getting enough reading done and, instead of going to bed early, had the idea of sharing someone else's candles.

'If we went over to William's each night,' he argued, 'you could see more of your sister and knit with her by the fire, and I could encourage William with his reading. He's a churchwarden, remember, and he needs to practise. I could help him. And it'll save on fuel.'

Elizabeth was disappointed. 'What about your father?' she asked. 'We can't leave him on his own.'

'I don't see why not. He never leaves his bed. He's safe enough.' Elizabeth raised her eyebrows. 'Anyway,' he went on, 'father sleeps most of the time. He wouldn't even know we were gone.'

Elizabeth was not convinced, but the next evening, and for many more that winter, they wrapped themselves up and waded through the snow to spend a few hours with William and Mary. Elizabeth grew very fond of young Francis and the boy looked forward to sitting on her knee and hearing nursery rhymes and songs. Usually he played for long periods by himself, talking to the wooden bowls and spoons which he liked to pile up and knock over. Now he began to say more words and string them together to make sense.

On such evenings, Kate found herself pushed to one side. When Elizabeth was there she was ignored and treated as a servant in the over-crowded kitchen; she was expected to sit further away from the fire and only approach when needed. She sat and sulked beneath the hams and flitches of bacon hanging under the rafters, wondering if she'd ever manage to save enough money to get married and live her own life.

While Kate brooded in the background, William and Robert shared a candle to pore over the Bible, and Mary and Elizabeth knitted by the fire. They used a yarn of coarse untreated wool, so full of lanolin it made their hands tacky at first but then silky smooth. They enjoyed their time together and gossiped about Susan and Simeon.

'I wonder,' said Elizabeth with a mischievous grin, 'how they'll ever manage with all this deep snow on the ground.'

Chapter 33

1709

The Gurwood girls also found comfort during the cold winter nights by huddling round the parlour fire and knitting. They sat on various stools and chairs surrounded by baskets of wool. Only the two youngest girls were allowed to be idle; the other six were kept busy by their mother who soon dealt with any complaints.

'I've told you before,' she said, not for the first time, 'you can't just knit for yourselves. It wouldn't be right. You're a vicar's daughters and you must knit for those less fortunate.'

'But why can't we sometimes knit something we can sell?' Cecilia asked. 'Then we'd have some money for ourselves.'

'Don't be selfish,' her mother replied. 'You're knitting for others and that's that.'

'Then why is Jane allowed to knit her own gloves?' Cecilia grumbled.

'You know very well. She'll be looking for suitors soon.'

Jane smiled at her mother and carried on clicking her needles, smug in the luxury of knitting for herself. She had two different balls of wool, black and white, to allow a pattern. Her needles were kept in her own knitting sheath, given on her seventeenth birthday, a very fine one made of beech and inlaid with bone. Her sisters had to make do with needles from their mother's sheath and were restricted to the simple stitches of knit one, purl one or, as their mother kept telling them, hit and miss it, hit and miss it. Despite the underlying ill grace, it was pleasant to sit by the fire together. Sometimes John would get his fiddle, and they'd sing to ward off their fears about the deepening frost outside.

By the end of January, the Gurwoods sat with as many clothes on as they could manage, as near to the fire as was safe and, even then, did not feel warm. John had the unwelcome experience of waking one morning to find his nightcap frozen to the bed-head. He couldn't shave because the water froze on his stubble before the razor could do its work and, when he cut his chin, his veins were so far below the skin that he hardly bled.

Water froze in the bowls and buckets and even Martha Wrench's ale froze in the casks. The ponds and wells, and the cistern at Uphall, all turned to ice; chunks had to be hacked off and melted over the fires. Dickon tried to make sure all the animals drank warm water but, by the time he carried it from the fire to the troughs, it had gone stone-cold again. Within minutes of pouring it out, ice would start creeping over the surface like ghostly fingers. The still air had almost a tinkling sound and, out in the yard, any noise carried for miles. At night, trees could be heard cracking apart as frost penetrated the trunks. Reighton, lying in a hollow, was trapped by the ice and snow. No one came into the village and no one left it.

For Susan and Simeon, the world had come to an end. At first, Simeon tried desperately to get to Susan, but no one would lend him a horse and, after once attempting to walk and getting stuck thigh-deep in drifts, he had to give up. Susan felt abandoned. She knew it was impossible for him to travel in such conditions yet experienced all the anger and bitterness of a scorned woman. Her whole family suffered and wished she'd never set eyes on him. Susan was confined, like everyone else, to living within reach of the fire. There was no escape from Isabella, her father and brothers, and the struggle of reining in her emotions and having to carry on as usual was beginning to tell on her nerves. She was not sleeping well either. The long nights in bed with Isabella were becoming unbearable. She used to enjoy feeling the warmth of her sister's body, had imagined it was Simeon asleep next to her; now it was just an annoying presence.

Stranded in Bartindale, Simeon was bored. He kicked around the yards teasing the other hired lads and tormenting any animals left defenceless in the sheds. It wasn't long before he found someone to flirt with and seduce. The milkmaid was, in Simeon's terms, a 'rough-lookin' scabby lass wi' no tits' but she was a woman and … when needs must … The poor girl was flattered by his attention and it wasn't long before he could do whatever he liked. They bedded down often in the hay loft above the stable and, in the dark, he could almost imagine she was pretty. She thought he was marvellous. He didn't think at all. He used her as he would a chamber pot.

In Reighton, Susan became more despondent as the ice showed no sign of thawing. She grew quieter and withdrew into herself as, like others, she felt the frustration and anger of weeks cooped up with only her family for company.

George Gurwood also found his patience tested more than usual by a house full of women. He often thought that God had strange ways of testing people – giving him eight daughters being one of the more insidious. They were always under his feet and never stopped chattering. When he huddled into a corner with a book, they assumed he was working on a sermon or reading a religious tract. He'd already decided, however, that it was far too cold to have church services and so was not going to waste time preparing sermons. The deep snow meant that no one could attend church anyway. Dressed in his quilted gown and with his thick woollen nightcap pulled over his shorn head, he edged his feet into his slippers and found a draught-free corner of the parlour. There he wrapped a woollen blanket round himself and settled down to escape into the wonderful world of *Don Quixote*.

The wildlife around Reighton continued to suffer from the great frost. Hardly any birds were seen in the sky and none were heard singing. The village became a silent, alien world where nothing was certain or as it should be. Jane Gurwood found that she could walk right up to birds and pick them up; they were too weak and cold to fly. One morning she brought a blackbird into the kitchen and warmed it by the fire. She managed to prise open its yellow beak and push in some bits of bread soaked in milk. When it revived and recovered enough to fly off, Jane's sisters began to look for other birds they could help. Soon, a variety of containers and baskets lay in a semicircle round the kitchen fire, each containing a bird or rabbit. Some birds became quite tame and perched on their hands to be fed. While the Gurwoods acted as good Samaritans, other villagers faced starvation and were less charitable. As the winter continued, any edible wildlife lying close to death was soon taken home for the pot.

Finally, in the middle of February, there was a thaw. For three days the snow melted. Although every field, lane and yard was knee-deep in mud and slush, everyone thought the worst was over. The winter wheat had been safe under the snow and they could now look forward to some spring weather. The thaw, however, only lasted for those three days and then the temperatures fell to below freezing again. It could not have been worse. Without the protection of the snow, the wheat was badly affected.

The freezing conditions lasted for another month. The ponds froze over again, the cart tracks turned into rock-hard ruts and the yards became slippery with ice. The side of the main street was so thick with black ice it was almost impossible to walk uphill. The children loved it. They made a slide that went right from the forge, round the corner past the vicarage and church, and only ended when it reached the small frozen mere at the bottom of St. Helen's Lane. And while the children played, the adults worried. They could not get any work done on the fields and feared for the future.

Chapter 34

At Uphall, Francis Jordan was fed up after spending so long indoors and decided to make another inspection of his tools and gear. Dickon, William and John stepped across the ice to join him, feeling their way gingerly along the walls. Francis fancied having a new plough made, or at least a new coulter as the metal was so worn as to be almost useless.

'Long, strong an' straight, eh?' Dickon said with a wink.

'Aye,' said Francis. 'It's what me father an' gran'father always used to say. Long, strong an' straight – then tha can plough a good furrow.' William and John rolled their eyes; their father always said the same when coulters were discussed. No doubt they'd be saying it to their own sons one day.

'Aye,' Francis repeated as he came to a decision. 'I'll speak to Phineas about a new coulter.'

However, when he spoke to the blacksmith, Phineas shook his head and pushed his horny hands under his apron. Francis watched him manoeuvre his hands inside his breeches. He had a habit of doing this whenever he was thinking. The blacksmith looked pensive as he fiddled about under his apron.

'I can't,' he replied at last. 'There's not enough iron – not sort tha needs for a coulter. I've run out. Look over yon.' He wriggled one hand free and waved towards the corner of his forge, normally full of supplies. It was quite bare. 'Wi' so much snow on roads, then ice, no one's fetchin' iron or coal fro' Bridlington. Carts keep gettin' stuck. They've all given up.'

When Francis returned to Uphall he explained the problem but had a solution. 'There's only one thing for it, lads – we'll 'ave to fetch iron ourselves.' William and John looked at each other, knowing the 'we' meant 'them'. Neither fancied a long ride and Dickon wouldn't want the horses out on the icy ground. An alternative was to use the oxen, but they'd be too slow.

William had an idea. 'We could put two of the horses in front, as pace setters, and four of the oxen behind. And fix the big sledge on. That might work. It's worth a try.'

'Best 'ave a word wi' Dickon then,' said his father. 'See what 'e 'as to say. Then wait for a calm day. Dickon'll make sure them 'orses get a good feed before they start.'

A week later the sun came out and the north wind eased. The ground remained frozen and Dickon prepared the harnesses and sledge. William and John were given extra porridge and their mother pushed a hot potato into their pockets.

'They'll keep tha warm,' she said, 'an' tha can eat 'em later.' She went to the fire and returned with a pot. 'I've melted this goose fat. Rub it well into tha faces. It'll stop tha gettin' chapped.' As they ate their porridge, she sat greasing their boots and then left them to warm by the fire. Before William and John pulled them on, she passed them some straw.

'Put this i' tha boots,' she ordered them. 'It'll stop cold comin' through.'

Outside in the cold stable, Tom had already caulked the horseshoes with oakum to give a better grip on the ice. He'd also fed both horses a ration of oats as well as hay. Now he was trying to warm the horses' bits. Afraid that the ice-cold metal would tear the tender skin of their mouths, he blew warm breath on the bits, and rubbed them vigorously between his hands.

When William and John stepped out into the bright early-morning sunshine, they noted that, during the night, there'd been another light fall of snow that had settled. Fresh piles of muck on the dung heap were steaming and, although the low sun was beginning to warm up the yard, it was still very cold in the shade by the walls. The horses stamped their feet restlessly as they were hitched to the oxen. William and John, wearing all their thickest clothes, mounted the horses with difficulty, and Dickon's fingers were numb as he fastened on the sledge. As they waved goodbye, their breath billowed like smoke.

They left the yard and headed south for Bridlington. Only the harness chains and the occasional cawing of a crow broke the silence. In the background they could just make out the distant roar of surf on the beach. William watched as rabbits scuffed away the snow, searching out any frosted blades of grass. The horses kept up a reasonable pace until they approached frozen puddles in the ruts, then one or both of them would stop and paw tentatively at the ice. After only half an hour of breathing in the icy air, William felt his chest tighten and begin to ache. His face was becoming sore and chapped despite the grease and, when he spoke to John, his voice sounded hoarse.

As they neared Bridlington the track deteriorated through overuse. There were deep holes and the sledge pitched sideways over the tops of old wheel ruts. The market area was deserted apart from a horde of raggedy children sliding down the road, but on the High Street the inns were doing a brisk trade. There was little to do except conduct business indoors and preferably over a meal and a pot of beer or two. William wanted to stop at The Seven Stars and enjoy a warm drink by the fire but knew he'd better keep the animals moving. Reluctantly, and with just the cooled potatoes to eat, they made their way to the harbour.

The winter weather had slowed business almost to a halt. Round the quay there were heaps of coal and timber and barrels of tar and salt, all awaiting buyers. They watered the animals and covered them with sacking before grabbing a quick drink and a pie at a tiny alehouse. It was warm inside, but they had to squash together at a table full of swearing harbour men smoking their pipes and waiting for work. Soon after midday, the temperature outside began to drop again and they daren't waste any more time. The traders at the quayside were more than pleased to sell some Dutch iron, so the deal was clinched quickly. The horses and oxen, now grown stiff and cold from inaction, stood like statues while the sledge was loaded.

The journey home was very slow since they'd not only bought iron for their own coulter, but iron for the whole village as well as candles and tar. By the time they reached Speeton, William thought he was frozen to his horse. He hadn't felt his legs for hours; they were just useless wooden appendages. The light was fading fast and it grew even colder as dusk approached.

Both William and John had been silent since leaving Bridlington. They accepted their suffering without complaint and clung onto the horses as best they could. Every step was one less to do, and one more that took them nearer home. John's face was almost hidden by his collar and the various cloths he'd wound about his neck and head. William's forehead was uncovered; it felt as if a clawed fist made of ice had grabbed it and dug in. He thought his head would split open with the cold, just as the ash tree near Uphall had been rent apart with the frost.

As they began their slow descent into Reighton, a fingernail paring of a moon shone down on them with one exceptionally bright star above it. A clear sky full of twinkling stars meant yet another night of below freezing temperatures. William wondered when the frost would end and whether it was some kind of judgement on them.

In the yard at Uphall, Tom was keeping watch for the returning sledge. As soon as he heard the jangling of the harnesses he ran to the kitchen and told Dorothy. She gave orders for the fire to be stoked up and blankets warmed while she dished out bowls of broth.

William and John were so numb with cold they had to be lifted from the horses. Neither of them could walk in a straight line and they stumbled, with Dickon's help, towards the lantern held at the doorway by their father. Tom and Dickon saw to the horses and oxen. The poor draught animals hadn't even realised they were home and looked about to give up. Dickon shuddered at the thought of losing them.

Inside the fuggy kitchen, Dorothy wanted to wrap her arms round her sons but, instead, spoke sharply. 'Get them boots off, John. Will, don't stand over there, come up closer to fire. That's it. John, don't leave tha boots there to freeze. Fetch 'em nearer fire. Lasses'll grease 'em again i' mornin'.'

Francis stared in admiration at his two sons. He was proud of their achievement but now anxious to know how much they'd brought back and how much they'd had to pay. William and John didn't want to talk. They slumped onto the settle near the fire and tried to warm their hands. Bowls of hot mutton broth were put in their laps but the warmth of the fire was making them drowsy. They couldn't keep their eyes open and just wanted to collapse and sleep – anywhere as long as it was warm.

William asked if someone could go over to Mary and tell her he'd be staying at Uphall for the night. At this, his mother smiled as she stirred the broth. She could hardly disguise her pleasure as she fished out more lumps of fatty mutton. It was good to have her eldest son back home, even if only for one night.

Chapter 35

By the end of February, William was sick of eating salted meat and smoked herrings. Food supplies were low and the meagre stores of peas, beans and oats were rationed even further. The poor harvest, coupled with the freezing winter, meant that before long they'd be mixing acorns with the grain to eke out the flour.

Having seen the success of the sledging trip to Bridlington, folk asked if William and John would make another trip to get salt and tobacco as well as extra food. The two brothers ended up making regular journeys. On one occasion they made an impulsive buy – a young mule at a bargain price. The size of a pony, its coat grey and shaggy, and with a mane stuck up straight like a donkey's, they soon found out why it was cheap. It kicked out in all directions and was startled by the slightest noise or movement. On the way home they faced numerous delays as the mule paused at every hole covered in ice. By the time they reached Uphall they were seriously regretting their purchase.

When Dickon saw the mule he rubbed the stubble on his chin, wondering how on earth he was going to look after it, let alone train it and, when the dogs in the yard barked and yelped round it, the mule went crazy. Dickon had to almost drag it, with Tom's help, to the back of the barn where they calmed it down eventually. Even then, they both risked being kicked. Once the dogs were back in the house, they led the mule to the stable, made a space for it and gave it food and water. Dickon was not happy and rushed to the house to complain.

'I don't know what Will an' John 'ad i' mind when they bought yon mule. Thoo should see it – a poor moth-eaten rag it looks. It can kick like a devil. Tom nearly lost 'is man'ood out there i' yard. Zounds! It's an evil thing.' Francis knew better than to interrupt. He let Dickon finish. 'I don't know as 'ow we can tend to it. An' what use is it? 'Ow can we train it? It's not like we're used to dealin' wi' such beasts.' Dickon fiddled with his hat, most aggrieved.

Francis promised he'd do something about it but, as yet, had no ideas. It was his wife who solved it in bed that night. It occurred to her that old Ben might be useful.

'I recall,' she said, 'as 'ow Ben used to look after some mules when 'e were young. Tha'd best get 'im to take a look at it. See what 'e says before everyone gives up on poor beast.'

The next morning Dickon called on Ben. Despite his faith in moles' feet, Ben's rheumatism had worsened in the damp, cold cottage and he hadn't been well all winter. He soon perked up on hearing the village now had a mule and walked with Dickon up the steep hill to Uphall faster than he'd done for months.

Inside the stable the mule looked very sorry for itself. Its head drooped and its eyes were half closed. Tom was standing well back, having just put food and water down. It certainly didn't look evil or capable of half of what it was accused. Nevertheless, Ben also stood well back. After a while he coughed as quietly as he could to clear his throat, and then spoke in a soft, husky voice.

'It's only a young un,' he decided, without daring to look in its mouth. 'What did tha want to do with 'er?' When Dickon explained that the mule would be a pack animal, if trained properly, Ben's eyes lit up and a broad smile transformed his weather-beaten face. He cleared his throat again. 'Listen, Dickon, I can train yon beast if I can take me time an' do what I thinks best. No one's to mess wi' mule except me. Agreed?' Dickon nodded, unable to believe his luck.

Tom winked at Dickon and put a hand on Ben's shoulder. 'Ben, thoo's a right expert, I can tell. Good luck to thee. That beast nearly 'ad me yesterday. Watch out for sideways kicks.'

'Thoo watch out, young Tom,' Ben grumbled. 'I can look after meself. It's all agreed then? Nobody but me touches yon mule?'

'Ben – she's all yours,' said Dickon with a huge grin. 'Do what tha likes. I'm sure Francis'll go along wi' whatever tha wants.'

From that day, Ben virtually lived in the stable. He slept there each night wrapped in a horse blanket by the side of the mule. He was better off there than in his own cottage; the stable was less draughty and he had the mule for company. He kept her as well-fed as he dared, knowing the shortages, and always spoke softly.

After a week he could groom her and lead her on a halter round the yard. The lads at Uphall had orders to stay away from Ben and the mule but they watched from a safe distance, either through the windows or from the sheds where they were mucking out. At the forge it was the main topic of conversation. How was Ben getting along with the mule? Was a marriage to be announced? They made jokes but had to respect Ben's patience and skill.

After another week, Ben brought in the saddle. He let her sleep next to it for a couple of nights and each morning he showed it to her and let her sniff it. All the while he talked non-stop and gazed at her like a lover. On the third morning he lifted the saddle onto her back, crooning all the time in his quiet, husky voice. He shifted the saddle around so that she could get used to the feel of it and then tied the girths loosely. The next day she let him saddle her up without fuss and he tightened the girths.

Folk were amazed to see Ben and the saddled mule walk sedately up and down the village. Ben introduced her to people and chatted to the mule as he escorted her round.

'Now, me lady,' he'd ask her, 'shall we 'ead on up to fields an' see Tom an' Dickon at work? Nay, not if tha doesn't wish it. Well then, shall we visit yon sheep?' And so they'd decide where to amble next. People asked what he called her.

'Patience!' said Ben. 'Princess Patience, I believe she'll be.' He held his head high, proud of his pupil. She was quiet and docile now, and only became restless when dogs were about.

By mid-March he'd added a harness and even accustomed her to a strap under her tail to keep the saddle steady. All that was needed now was to introduce some kind of a load. He began by adding a couple of bags of sand, and then tried a variety of items and weights. He always let her see and smell the load before attempting to lift it onto her back and was careful not to make her strain herself going up steep hills. Though she was ready for proper work, he delayed the moment. Instead, he spent days training her to walk over different terrains and jump over small ditches. He always kept the reins slack and never used a whip.

At the forge, the blacksmith laughed at Ben as he went by. ''Ow long will it be,' he shouted, 'before tha tries yon mule in a steeplechase?' Ben ignored him.

Towards the end of March, when the great thaw began, Ben declared that Patience could now begin to earn her keep. Tom was chosen as the lad to be in charge so long as he always deferred to Ben. He spent time learning how best to handle her, and Ben shadowed them for a while and gave advice.

'Listen, lad – tha must avoid dogs, speak gently to 'er an' only move at a steady pace, don't rush. An' never forget to balance what loads tha puts o' saddle.'

The choice of Tom was a good one as he treated the mule much like he treated the young Jordan children; he couldn't force them to do things either but, with a little cajoling and gentle persuasion, they'd be butter in his hands. After a few short trips with the mule, Tom came to appreciate her intelligence. He realised that any stubbornness or disobedience was due only to her instinct for self-preservation. He began to trust her judgement, knowing she'd always pick the easiest, safest route and would adopt the most suitable pace for the conditions. The mule was a godsend, giving Tom a new interest in life.

Ben's job was done, however, and he'd lost his companion. Patience would now have to bond with someone else. He missed her and visited every day. Ben would often be found in the stable talking away to the mule, telling her all the details of his repetitive daily life.

The wet spring, however, gave Ben a new preoccupation. He'd always been a keen observer of the weather and used the behaviour of his bees to make forecasts. Lately, with more time on his hands, he'd become obsessed with his predictions and was never happier than when he left his cottage with exactly the right clothing for the day's weather. This obsession led to experiments. He was determined to create the ultimate in waterproof headwear. Having suffered from earache in windy weather, the 'hat' would also need to cover his ears and keep them warm. William found him one morning knitting the last part of a tremendously long, thin woollen strip which, Ben said, was to be wound round his head like a bandage. Ben finished the strip and asked William to help him bind it on.

'Mind tha covers me ears. That's main job of it.'

'Aye, don't fret. Your ears are well-covered. I bet you can't hear me now, can you, you old fool?'

'I 'eard that, young rapscallion.'

'There, it's done.' William tucked in the loose end.

'Now we 'ave to lift it off, careful like, i' one go. Steady! Steady, lad.' It came off his head in one piece like a mould. 'Now I'm goin' to dip it i' yon tar.'

William was doubtful and watched, unimpressed, as the woollen mould, shaped like a pudding-basin, acquired a waterproof skin of tar. He tried not to grin too broadly but it looked ridiculous. He guessed it would serve its purpose; when it rained, Ben's head would stay both warm and dry.

Ben had always liked messing about with tar and often stank of the stuff, but his passion for tar products at least kept the village stocked with fire-lighters. He spent whole mornings dipping lengths of flax in tar and winding them round sticks. From time to time, children were sent to fetch a bundle of these links. He made sure to give them advice, usually about the weather.

'Tha's to try an' love all weathers,' he told them. 'Rain, snow, wind an' sun, an' tha must also welcome grey an' dull days. They all come round. They all take their turn. None of 'em lasts.'

The children passed this advice on to their parents, but it was hard to take after suffering three months of frost. Ben's philosophy was put to the test again in late March when, instead of spring sunshine and drying winds, they faced torrential rain.

Chapter 36

The fierce rain storms and the melting ice from the hills brought floods. Quagmires appeared everywhere. One day towards the end of March, William and John were sheltering inside the barn with all the hired lads. The rain was so heavy they couldn't hear themselves speak or see further than the grey curtain of water that had suddenly descended. After over two months of idleness and trying to keep warm indoors they were now faced with the prospect of waterlogged fields and impassable tracks. When it did finally stop raining, they peered out onto the flooded yard where the ducks and geese squabbled. The troughs were overflowing, and rust-coloured water leached from the wood piles and stained the yard. At least the birds had begun to sing again but it was hard to believe that spring was really on its way.

William stood with his hands deep in his coat pockets, his shoulders hunched up. He worried about the state of the hay meadow now lying well under water. No hay this year meant no food for the oxen and therefore no fuel to drive the plough, therefore no sowing and no crops, therefore starvation and ruin. Another worry was the hay supply from last year which had shrunk almost to nothing. It looked like more animals would have to be slaughtered.

Spring arrived very late. Instead of warmer weather, they had more rain to contend with. Rain. They were sick of hearing the word. They saw every kind of rain that 'spring' – the fine haze that gradually seeped into everything; the cold, pouring rain under low grey skies that seemed never-ending and made the fields soggy; the driving rain that came with the northeast wind and drilled through walls, found gaps in the window frames and left puddles all around the house; and, finally, the most common of rains – a steady, gentle drizzle throughout the day, only stopping at night when they couldn't go out to work.

Susan Jordan was suffering more than most. She had a painful, physical longing for the spring. When she realised that Simeon could never get over to Reighton now because of the mud, she lost all control. The pent-up emotions of her long winter indoors exploded suddenly in early April. It was the lice and dirty clothes that proved to be the last straw. All winter the family had been plagued by lice and they were all dying to have a good wash and launder their linen. Susan couldn't stop itching and fretted constantly about her appearance, wanting to look her best, just in case. One morning at breakfast she'd scratched herself raw without realising what she was doing. When she noticed the mess on her arms and chest she screamed.

'Oh my God! Oh God! I can't stand anymore. I can't stand it.' She got up and ran round the kitchen table pulling at her cap strings and muttering over and over, 'I can't stand it. I can't stand it.'

Isabella slapped her face. Her brothers just looked on, their spoons halfway to their mouths, wondering what on earth was the matter. Susan covered her face with her hands and began to sob. Her chest heaved and shuddered as she gasped for breath. Isabella made her sit down. Between the sobs, Susan complained about the dirty house, the lice, the weather, her family, and the scuffling mice that kept her awake at night. They sympathised, but they'd had to endure it as well and they weren't demented. Nothing would console her. On her father's instructions, Isabella put Susan to bed and then went to Sarah Ezard for a sleeping draught.

While Susan slept feverishly, Isabella sat at her father's bedside. She told him about Simeon. That was Susan's main problem, she explained, and there was no way of helping her. He swore and spat on the floor. To him, Simeon was at best a nobody, at worst a scoundrel. There was going to be an end to it. He checked later with his sons that Isabella's story was correct, never quite trusting what a woman said. When they added more details to confirm it, he demanded to be taken to see the vicar. The boys could carry him there if necessary. Isabella could not dissuade him so made sure he was well wrapped up and, with a son on each side, he managed to walk to the vicarage.

After wiping their boots on the scraper they were led into the parlour. John Gurwood reddened when he saw Susan's father and vacated the room quickly with his sisters.

'Good morning, David,' began the vicar. 'It must be important for you to come out in this weather.'

'Aye, I'm all mixed up. Don't know what to do for best, like.'

The vicar showed him to a chair by the fire. They sat opposite each other while the two sons stood by, awkward and out of place, trying not to leave mud on the carpet.

'Take your time,' coaxed the vicar. 'I'll help if I can, God willing.'

After staring into the fire for a few moments, David Jordan looked up, swallowed hard and began to pour out his worries.

'It's Susan. Like all of us, she's suffered bad this winter.' He stopped and twisted in his chair. He looked again at the fire, embarrassed about what he had to report. 'I know she were fond o' thy John. I thought as 'ow 'e'd maybe lost interest.' He saw that George Gurwood looked puzzled. 'Any'ow,' he continued, 'to cut a long story short like … she were seein' Simeon.' He glanced quickly at George to gauge his reaction and then went on. 'I never knew about it, like, thoo understands. Never knew a thing. Not till this mornin'.'

'I'm sorry, David. I didn't know. I hardly know my own children sometimes. They have a way of leading you in the wrong direction when it comes to their affairs.'

'Maybe so, but it's my Susan that's sufferin' like. This mornin' she were beside 'erself. Isabella 'ad to put 'er to bed. We couldn't do nowt with 'er.'

'If you like, I'll pay a visit. I could say a few prayers and maybe that would calm her. From what I've heard of Simeon and his effect on women, you might be needing all your patience and charity.'

David Jordan raised his eyebrows and looked at George. He lifted his arms up high, as if to call on God's help, before letting them fall heavily again to his sides.

George pleaded with him. 'Don't be too hard on her, David. It might take time for her to get over Simeon.'

'I'm not 'avin' it. Soon as she sorts 'erself out, she's leavin', the young gammerstags.'

'Are you sure that'll be for the best?'

'Best for everyone as far as I can see. Look 'ere – Simeon's at Bartindale. We're too near for 'im. As soon as weather's cleared 'e'll be sniffin' round 'ere again after Susan. Nay … she's leavin'.'

'Don't decide on anything yet, David. Let me see her first and then we'll talk about it again.'

Word soon went round the village that Susan was confined to her bed and in a poor state of health. As her sister remarked, she was like a young bird with a broken wing. When Susan did manage to drag herself out of bed, she traipsed round the kitchen and showed no interest in either cooking or eating. At night, when Susan couldn't sleep, Isabella warmed up a linen bag filled with nutmeg, mace and treacle and laid it on her sister's temples. The whole family was now sorry for Susan and anxious for her recovery.

Sarah Ezard did her best; she brought tea made with agrimony and rosemary to lift Susan's melancholy and chanted rhymes in case it was the devil at work taking advantage of weakness and misfortune. Nutritious food was scarce that spring and, while everyone was low and lacking in energy, Susan had no mental reserves to sustain her. She was worn out physically and emotionally – and also spiritually, as George Gurwood discovered.

The vicar called round more when he heard that Susan was out of bed. He made a habit of sitting beside her to read the Bible and always ended his visits by saying The Lord's Prayer. She never acknowledged him or joined in but he persevered in spite of her dark, sullen looks. Any expression was an improvement on her blank stare.

However, as the weather brightened, she grew excitable and was feverish again at night. Isabella sensed Susan's rising hopes and was afraid of a relapse. All the potions and prayers had amounted to nothing. It was time for a different remedy, and Susan's father believed the time had come to be more practical. One day, as the vicar was leaving, he complained to him.

'It's no good. Susan i'n't recoverin'. She needs summat else.'

They mulled over alternative courses of action. David was adamant that Susan had brought shame on the whole family and needed to be further away from Simeon.

'She's useless to me now,' he argued. 'She's useless to 'erself. Nay – there 'as to be some big change. Can't tha do summat? I want 'er out of 'ere. Does tha know of anywhere I can send 'er?'

George said he'd think about it and let him know by the end of the week.

'Don't take too long, vicar. Susan's gettin' fidgety now warmer weather's 'ere. Tha knows who'll come runnin' an' we'll be back where we started.'

George Gurwood discussed the problem with his son. John had loved Susan once and then hated her but was now genuinely sad that she was to leave Reighton in this manner. He suggested they try the Stutville family. Although Charles Stutville lived rather close by in Hunmanby, he had a large five-hearthed house with six main rooms as well as garrets. An extra servant might well be required there and Susan would be kept under strict discipline. Even if Simeon discovered her whereabouts he would think twice before daring to visit her there. George Gurwood agreed it could be the answer.

As soon as Susan was feeling stronger, her father told her the plan. She screamed with a wild look in her eyes as if about to attack him, but he'd planned his moment well. Susan's two brothers stepped up from behind and held her by the arms. Isabella appeared with a large bag packed with Susan's few clothes and possessions. None of them dared disobey their father; he looked as if he might have a heart attack. The horse was waiting outside. Susan screamed again as she was carried off her feet. She stuck her legs out in the doorway to try and wedge herself there, but her brothers were too strong and soon forced her through.

The drizzle and the cold morning air shocked her into realising she was outside and people could see her. She allowed herself to be lifted onto the horse. Richard led the way slowly down the village and onto the shortest track for Hunmanby. There were no goodbyes. She left in silence. Once out of the village, she let the tears fall. Richard had no words of comfort to give her – he was just following his father's instructions. He was more concerned with the weather, with how much it might rain today.

Back in Reighton, Isabella was already getting on with her chores. Now, as the only woman in the house, she felt rather grand; she was also lonely and wondered, after betraying Susan, if she'd ever see her again.

Chapter 37

The rain continued throughout the spring. Pastures remained waterlogged and cart ruts full to the brim with dark puddles. The rain found new ways to trickle into buildings and all the tools were damp. The cattle, now out in the fields but restricted to the higher ground, stood sheltering near the hedges, their cold, wet backs hunched up and tense. The sea turned a filthy, muddy brown as the tides and rain combined to erode the cliffs, and the leaden-grey clouds, as if in sympathy with everyone's spirits, hung low over the village.

Ben's rheumatism played up more in the damp weather. Sarah Ezard, not liking to see him suffer, made up a special concoction. She weighed out a pound of the blackest flint stones and pounded them into small pieces. Then she boiled them over a slow fire in a couple of pints of milk that she'd procured fresh from Uphall. Ben was to drink half a pint each bedtime for four nights and also keep out of the cold. Whether the medicine or just being warmer did the trick, Ben was soon well enough to walk up and down the village again. On hearing that Robert Storey's father lay ill with a bad cough, he went to the house with advice.

'Robert,' he said sternly, 'listen. Thoo needs to rub tha father's chest wi' goose fat. It's always worked for me whenever I've been wheezy.' Robert thanked him. He wanted to do what was best.

That night, he got out the goose fat. His father was now so bony and frail that he daren't rub too hard. It alarmed both him and Elizabeth when the old man couldn't get his breath. Neither of them fancied Sarah Ezard's 'cure' of smoking a pipe of dried coltsfoot leaves. They believed the problem was the winter build-up of smoke in the house. After some consultation with her mother, Elizabeth started giving her father-in-law a small spoonful of cod liver oil twice a day. Although he didn't breathe any better, he didn't deteriorate either, and Robert and Elizabeth thought they were over the worst.

The extended bad weather meant that Sarah Ezard soon ran out of the rosemary salve they all used for the lice and nits. Now people had to run a lighted candle along the seams of their clothes. They heard, with satisfaction, the hard shells of the lice crack under the heat and felt they'd gained some control over the vermin. Sarah spent most of each day visiting the sick, handing out her horehound and honey cough mixture and prescribing a willow bark infusion for all the aches and pains brought on by the damp climate.

George Gurwood kept the village informed of the country's progress in the war, despite thinking that the problem over the Spanish Succession was rather remote and unlikely to appeal to his congregation. Three times a week, as a dutiful Anglican vicar, he read out prayers written in London and sent out 'in time of war and tumults'.

One afternoon he discussed the latest news with his son, John. They lit their pipes and settled down by the parlour fire, appreciating the rarity of having the room to themselves. They drew contentedly on their pipes, enjoying the peace and quiet.

'It seems our armies have had some success,' George said at last to break the silence. 'Ghent and Bruges have been much reduced and we've taken Lisle.'

John puffed away at his pipe, happy to be alone with his father and no sisters present. 'Is there some hope then of us making peace with France?' he asked after a while.

'I think King Louis might be facing defeat now, but don't forget it's his own grandson on the Spanish throne and he's ambitious. He's not going to give up easily.'

'Is it true,' John said with a grin, 'that the French king sees his advisers while he sits on his privy closet?'

'That's what I've heard.' They laughed together and stretched their feet towards the fire. They didn't say it, but both were well aware that the successes of the English and their allies would be small consolation in Reighton after the cruel winter and the wet spring.

The next time George Gurwood stood in the pulpit he looked down on his flock with pity. After an inactive winter indoors, eking out supplies or simply going without, everyone was pale and thin and quite unfit for work. He knew what old Ben would call them – 'nowt but a bunch o' windlestraws.'

Mary sat in her pew feeling weaker than usual. She'd missed her bleeding for two months in a row. This could have been due to loss of weight over the winter but she guessed, from her changeable moods, that she was with child again. She decided to wait a bit longer before telling William, just in case.

The wet spring turned into a misty, hot summer. Late crops managed to do well, but the cereal crops were a disaster. All year folk had been bulking out their meagre supplies of meal with nettles and thistles. Sarah Ezard had even made a kind of flour powder by grinding ferns. It didn't help when George Gurwood told them that people in France were so hungry they'd eaten grass.

Old Ben was mystified by the weather. He knew that a harsh winter meant a good summer, yet this year it was not the case. It was dry for weeks when they needed rain; it was damp and misty when the hay was ready for cutting; it was windy just before harvest time and the scant crops were flattened. All anyone could do now was put their faith in God and hope for the best.

George Gurwood was having doubts about the efficacy of prayer and found himself referring more and more to his worn copy of Marcus Aurelius. Aware of his duty as a vicar, he attempted to bolster up flagging spirits.

'Do not moan and grumble about your fate,' he exhorted them in church on Sunday. 'Do not chafe against nature and your destiny – that would be to rebel against God.'

He knew it was a lot to ask but continued in the same vein. 'Be content with what you have. Trust in God's providence and welcome gladly all that befalls you. Welcome the weather sent you. Face it undaunted and know it's part of the natural order of things. We should see life as a gift and live out our appointed lot with grace.' The people sitting below had no option but to suffer and get through the rest of the year as well as they were able.

The anniversary of Anna Jordan's death at the end of August turned everyone's thoughts once more to their allotted spans on this earth and the mysterious workings of God. In church they heard about the defeat of the French army at Malplaquet. George Gurwood hoped this victory would raise their morale. They had a new hero, John Churchill, Duke of Marlborough, who had led the allied forces. George did not reveal that the heavy casualties meant the Tories were now calling Marlborough 'the Butcher'. He need not have worried unduly. Such news hardly affected his flock. He understood that life was precarious at best, and a distant victory in some foreign place was not going to make much difference. Life in Reighton would continue – a struggle as always with the weather.

He read of the introduction of the 'hoop petticoat' into London fashions and considered this yet another calamity. At least Reighton, and therefore his daughters, would be unaffected by the new fashion for some time. He still wanted an end to 1709 before anything worse could happen. He was well aware that some were dealing with more impending issues; old Roger Storey was very ill and Mary Jordan was with child again.

Towards the middle of December, Mary went into labour and, in the presence of only her mother, Sarah Ezard and Kate, gave birth to a small girl. As soon as Mary was settled with the baby and all appeared well, Kate put on her winter cloak and almost ran to Uphall with the news. It was the middle of the afternoon and she found William in the yard with Dickon.

'I've got some good news for thee,' she shouted as she approached. 'Mary's 'ad 'er bairn. It's a girl.'

'Congratulations, lad,' Dickon said and gave William a rough handshake. William was shocked. When he'd left Mary at breakfast time there'd been no hint of an imminent birth. Now he'd have to stay at Uphall for Christmas. When Dickon walked off to the stable, Kate could see that William was upset.

'Tha gander month'll soon pass,' she said. 'Thoo'll be back 'ome soon.' Thinking she'd spoken out of turn, she rushed off, leaving him to come to terms with the news.

That evening after supper, William couldn't wait to see Mary and his new daughter. His mother was against the idea of him visiting and tried to put him off.

'Thoo'll bring bad luck visitin' so early.' When he fetched the large lantern and pulled on his boots she gave in. 'Don't hearken to me then. Do what tha will, but God 'elp thee.' Before he left the house she shouted, 'An' don't forget to wrap summat round tha boots – it's slippy with ice out there.'

William stepped out into the frosty night to see a sky full of stars. He hesitated before lighting the lantern and stood for a while in the cold, clear air. As he took a deep breath he thought that things could change, could get better. A new life had started and a new year was just round the corner. With shaking hands he lit the lantern and trod carefully out of the yard, avoiding ice where he could.

The descent towards St. Helen's Lane was tricky; more than once he slipped and wondered if he should be doing this. Maybe his mother was right, but he could not have sat in peace at Uphall. Ever since he'd heard the news he'd been on tenterhooks. He didn't know why he was so fidgety. Maybe it was because he hadn't expected the birth so soon, or perhaps it was because it was a winter baby. The others had all been born in the middle of summer. His heart thudded as he approached the lane. He prayed that both mother and child would be well.

On reaching his house he knocked lightly on the door in case of waking Mary. Kate let him in, only a little surprised by the visit.

'Mary's still awake,' she said. 'Go through, but wait – take tha coat an' boots off first.' He was forgetting in his hurry and was almost in the parlour. Kate watched him fumble with his buttons and decided to help him with his boots.

He tiptoed into the parlour, dark except for one candle burning near the bed. Mary smiled and pointed to the crib. The baby girl was so swaddled up, only her face was visible. She was asleep and her lips parted as she breathed. Something seemed to melt inside him. He had a desperate desire to protect this little girl, make her life happy and free of worry. He didn't know why this baby should affect him so. He'd had a daughter before, though she hadn't survived long. Forcing himself to believe it would be different this time, he took the baby gently from the crib and held her in his arms.

Mary saw his radiant face in the candlelight, the soft glazed-over look in his eyes that he'd reserved in the past for her. With a slight pang of jealousy she offered words of caution.

'Middle of December's not the best time to have a baby.'

He ignored her and walked towards the window, pulled back the curtain and held the baby up. 'Look out there, little Mary. See the garden white with frost? See it sparkle in the moonlight? I'll take you up the hill one day. We'll see the sheep and you can meet Dickon and Tom. There's old Ben as well – he'll tell you some tales. You're going to have such a lovely life.' He kissed her forehead.

His eyes were wet as he turned back to his wife. He sat on the bed, the baby still in his arms and spoke with conviction.

'Don't forget – the babies we lost were born in summer. This time it's different, you'll see. Our luck will change.'

Book Two

New Arrivals

1709 to 1714

The November hirings bring trouble when a good-looking brother and sister come to Uphall. Both Jordan girls are smitten. Summer bonfires, wassailing and Twelfth Night festivities give plenty of opportunity for the girls to promote their cause and outwit their rival.

William and Mary Jordan's marriage is tested as the family grows. Their daughter, young Mary, proves more than a handful. She's lively, precocious and totally fearless as everyone in Reighton is about to find out.

About the Author

Joy Stonehouse is born and bred in the East Riding. Her maternal forebears were Jordans from Reighton.